MILES TO
Go

**Center Point
Large Print**

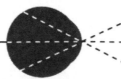

MILES TO *Go*

THE SECOND JOURNAL OF *THE WALK*

RICHARD PAUL EVANS

CENTER POINT LARGE PRINT
THORNDIKE, MAINE

This Center Point Large Print edition is
published in the year 2011 by arrangement with
Simon & Schuster, a division of Simon & Schuster, Inc.

The text of this Large Print edition is unabridged.
In other aspects, this book may vary
from the original edition.
Printed in the United States of America.
Set in 16-point Times New Roman type.

ISBN: 978-1-61173-067-8

Library of Congress Cataloging-in-Publication Data

Evans, Richard Paul.
 Miles to go / Richard Paul Evans.
 p. cm.
 ISBN 978-1-61173-067-8 (lib. bdg. : alk. paper)
 1. Executives—Fiction. 2. Life change events—Fiction.
    3. Voyages and travels—Fiction.
    4. Walking—United States—Fiction. 5. Loss (Psychology)—Fiction.
    6. Identity (Psychology)—Fiction. 7. Large type books. I. Title.
 PS3555.V259M55 2011
 813'.54—dc22

                                                    2011005383

ACKNOWLEDGMENTS

I thank the following for their assistance on this book: My daughter Jenna, for her wisdom, editorial advice and endurance on the road. It was Jenna's idea on where to end this story. I'm proud of you, honey.

Laurie Liss, just for being you. Dr. Steve Schlozman for helping me at such a difficult time. Jonathan Karp, for your enthusiasm for this series. Gypsy da Silva, Karen Thompson and Amanda Murray, for editorial advice. Liz Peterson and Chris Evans—for helping us find our way around Spokane. Kailamai Hansen. Kelly Glad, thanks for always being ready with an answer. Pattie Servine, P.R. Department at Sacred Heart Medical Center. Taylor Swift just because I really like your music. Carl Evans and Detective Corbett Ford of the Cottonwood Heights Police Department. Tony Bonney.

And the crew of the *Windstar*, especially Amanda Millar, who delivered the proofs of this book in Virgin Gorda, miraculously.

My staff: Diane Glad, Barry Evans, Heather McVey, Fran Plat, Lisa Johnson, Lisa McDonald, Sherri Engar, Jed Platt, and Doug Smith.

The family; Keri, Jenna and David, Allyson, Abigail, McKenna and Michael.

As always, my Heavenly Father.

To Karen Christoffersen

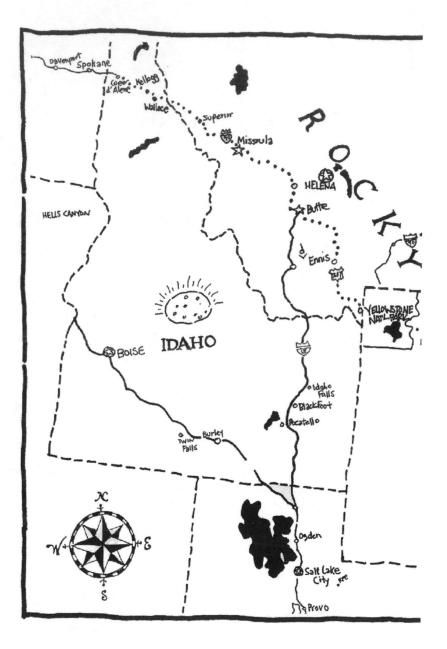

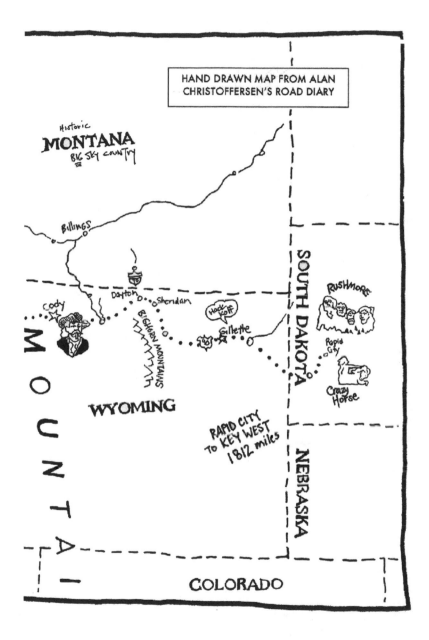

HAND DRAWN MAP FROM ALAN
CHRISTOFFERSEN'S ROAD DIARY

Historic
MONTANA
BIG SKY COUNTRY

Billings

Cody

Dayton

Sheridan

BIGHORN MOUNTAINS

Hold
KOFF

Gillette

WYOMING

M O U N T A I

SOUTH DAKOTA

RUSHMORE

Rapid
City

Crazy
Horse

RAPID CITY
TO KEY WEST
1812 miles

NEBRASKA

COLORADO

Stopping by Woods on a Snowy Evening

Whose woods these are I think I know.
His house is in the village, though;
He will not see me stopping here
To watch his woods fill up with snow.

My little horse must think it queer
To stop without a farmhouse near
Between the woods and frozen lake
The darkest evening of the year.

He gives his harness bells a shake
To ask if there is some mistake.
The only other sound's the sweep
Of easy wind and downy flake.

The woods are lovely, dark, and deep,
But I have promises to keep,
And miles to go before I sleep,
And miles to go before I sleep.

—Robert Frost

MILES TO

Go

PROLOGUE

*The sun will rise again. The only
uncertainty is whether or not
we will rise to greet it.*

Alan Christoffersen's diary

Several months after I was mugged, stabbed, and left unconscious along the shoulder of Washington's Highway 2, a friend asked me what being stabbed felt like. I told her it hurt.

Really, how do you describe pain? Sometimes doctors ask us to rate our pain on a scale from one to ten, as if that number had some reliable meaning. In my opinion there needs to be a more objective rating system, something comparative; like, would you trade what you're feeling for a root canal or maybe half a childbirth?

And with what would we compare emotional pain—physical pain? Arguably, emotional pain is the greater of the two evils. Sometimes people will inflict physical pain on themselves to dull their emotional anguish. I understand. If I had the choice between being stabbed or losing my wife, McKale, again, the knife has the advantage —because if the knife kills me, I stop hurting. If it doesn't kill me, the wound will heal. Either way the pain stops. But no matter what I do, my McKale is never coming back. And I can't imagine that the pain in my heart will ever go away.

Still, there is hope—not to forget McKale, nor even to understand why I had to lose her—but to accept that I did and somehow go on. As a friend recently said to me, no matter what I do, McKale will always be a part of me. The question is, what part—a spring of gratitude, or a fountain of bitterness? Someday I'll have to decide. Someday the sun will rise again. The only uncertainty is whether or not I will rise to greet it.

In the meantime, what I hope for most is *hope*. Walking helps. I wish I were walking again right now. I think I'd rather be anywhere right now than where I am.

CHAPTER
One

We plan our lives in long, unbroken
stretches that intersect our dreams the
way highways connect the city dots on
a road map. But in the end we learn
that life is lived in the side roads,
alleys, and detours.

Alan Christoffersen's diary

My name is Alan Christoffersen and this is the
second journal of my walk. I'm writing from a
hospital room in Spokane, Washington. I'm not
sure how you came to be holding my book—
truthfully, I don't even know if you are—but if
you're reading my story, welcome to my journey.

You don't know much about me. I'm a thirty-
two-year-old former advertising executive, and
sixteen days ago I walked away from my home in
Bridle Trails, Seattle, leaving everything behind,
which, frankly, wasn't much by the time I started
my trek. I'm walking to Key West, Florida—that's
about 3,500 miles, give or take a few steps.

Before my life imploded, I was, as one of my
clients put it, "the poster child for the American
dream"—a happily married, successful advertising
executive with a gorgeous wife (McKale), a

thriving advertising agency with a wall of awards and accolades, and a $2 million home with horse property and two luxury cars parked in the garage.

Then the universe switched the tracks beneath me, and in just five weeks I lost it all. My slide began when McKale broke her neck in a horse-riding accident. Four weeks later she died of complications. While I was caring for her in the hospital, my clients were stolen by my partner, Kyle Craig, and my financial world collapsed, leading to the foreclosure of my home and repossession of my cars.

With my wife, business, house, and cars gone, I packed up what I needed to survive and started my walk to Key West.

I'm not trying to set any records or wind up in any newspapers. I'm certainly not the first to cross the continent by foot; I'm at least a century too late for that. In fact, the first attempt was made more than two hundred years ago by a man named John Ledyard, who planned to walk across Siberia, ride a Russian fur-trade vessel across the ocean to (what is now) Alaska, and then walk the rest of the way to Washington, D.C., where Thomas Jefferson would warmly greet him. Such are the plans of men. Ledyard only made it as far as Siberia, where Russian Empress, Catherine the Great, had him arrested and sent to Poland.

Since then, no less than a few thousand pioneers, prospectors, and mountainmen have crossed the continent without air-cushioned walking shoes, paved roads, or, unbelievably, a single McDonald's.

Even in our day there is a sizable list of country-crossers, including an eighty-nine-year-old woman who walked from California to Washington, D.C., and a New Jersey man who *ran* from New Brunswick to San Francisco in exactly sixty days.

Nearly all of these travelers carried causes with them, from political reform to childhood obesity. Not me. The only torch I'm carrying is the one for my wife.

You might guess that my destination was chosen for its balmy weather, blinding white beaches, and topaz blue waters, but you'd be wrong: Key West was simply the furthest point on the map from where I started.

I should add the disclaimer that Key West is my *intended* destination. It is my experience that journeys rarely take us where we think we're going. As Steinbeck wrote, "we do not take a trip; a trip takes us." There's a difference between reading a map and traveling the road—as distinct as the disparity between reading a menu and eating a meal. So it is with life. As the saying goes, "Life is what happens to us while we're planning something else." That is true. Even my detours had detours.

My most recent detour has left me in the emergency room of Sacred Heart Medical Center with a concussion and three knife wounds to my belly after being jumped by a gang three miles outside Spokane. That's where you're joining me.

For those of you who have been following my walk since my first step (or before), I warned you that my story wouldn't be easy. I suppose that's no surprise; no one's story is easy. No one goes through life without pain—of this I'm certain. The price for joy is sadness. The price for having is loss. You can moan and whine about this and play the victim—many do—but it's just the way it is. I've had a lot of time to think about this. That's one of the benefits of walking.

I also warned you in my first journal that you might not believe or be ready for all I have to share with you. This book is no different. No matter—accept or dismiss what you want to believe.

Since I began my walk, I've traveled only 318 miles, less than ten percent of the distance to Key West. But already there have been profound experiences; I've met people along the way I believe I was meant to meet and I'm certain there are more to come.

This is a story of contrasts—about living and dying, hope and despair, pain and healing, and the tenuous, thin places between both extremes where most of us reside.

I'm not sure whether I'm walking away from my past or toward a future—time and miles will tell and I have plenty of both. As the poet Robert Frost said, I have "miles to go before I sleep."

I'm happy to share with you what I learn. Welcome to my walk.

CHAPTER
Two

I've gone from a schedule of hours
and minutes to not being able to tell
you what day of the month it is.

Alan Christoffersen's diary

My second night in the hospital was rough. I was wet and hot with fever and somewhere in the night I started coughing. Each expulsion felt like another blade plunging into my stomach. The nurse checked my bandages, then told me not to cough, which wasn't at all helpful. In spite of the medications they gave me to help me sleep, for most of the night I just lay there, lonely and aching. I wanted McKale more than life. Definitely more than life. Of course, if she were with me, I wouldn't be in this mess in the first place. Exhaustion finally overcame me and I fell asleep around 4 or 5 A.M.

The next day I woke to a young nurse walking around my bed looking at monitors and writing on a clipboard. Since I'd been admitted to the hospital, a bevy of nurses and doctors had been swarming around me in my delirium, flashing in and out of my consciousness like dancers in a music video. But I didn't remember any of them.

This was the first nurse I was cognizant of. She was small, petite, and barely the height of a floor lamp. I watched her for a few minutes then said, "Morning."

She looked up from her clipboard. "Good afternoon."

"What time is it?" I asked. It was kind of a funny question since I didn't even know what day, or week, it was. The last two weeks had run together like eggs in a blender.

"It's almost twelve-thirty," she said, then added, "Friday."

Friday. I had left Seattle on a Friday. I'd been gone for just fourteen days. Fourteen days and a lifetime.

"What's your name?"

"I'm Norma," she said. "Are you hungry?"

"How about an Egg McMuffin?" I said.

She grinned. "Not unless you can find one made of Jell-O. How about some pudding? The butterscotch is edible."

"Butterscotch pudding for breakfast?"

"Lunch," she corrected. "Also, in a couple hours we're sending you in for a CT scan."

"When can I take the catheter out?"

"When you can walk to the bathroom on your own—which we'll attempt after we get the results back from your scan. Are you claustrophobic?"

"No."

23

"Sometimes people get claustrophobic in the scanner. I can give you something for anxiety if you are. A Valium."

"I don't need anything," I said. I didn't care about the scan; I wanted the catheter out of me. In the haze of the last forty-eight hours, I vaguely remembered pulling the catheter out and making a real mess of things.

I had two good reasons for wanting it out; first, because it hurt. No one should stick any-thing up that part of the male anatomy. Second, an infection from a catheter is what killed my wife. The sooner the thing was out, the better.

A hospital orderly, a husky young freckled man wearing bright purple scrubs, came for me around two in the afternoon. He unhooked some wires and tubes from my body, then wheeled my entire bed down the linoleum corridor to radiology. I didn't know it was my second visit until the technician operating the equipment said, "Welcome back."

"Have I been here before?"

"You were out the first time," she replied.

The scan was tedious, surprisingly loud, and took about an hour. When it was through, the orderly wheeled me back to my room and I fell asleep. When I woke, Angel was back.

CHAPTER
Three

Somewhere between being stabbed and waking in the hospital, I had an experience that's difficult to describe. Call it a dream or a vision, but McKale came to me. She told me that it wasn't my time to die—that there were still people I was meant to meet. When I asked her who, she replied, "Angel." Who is this woman?

Alan Christoffersen's diary

The first time I woke in the hospital, there was a strange woman sitting in a chair next to my hospital bed. She was about my age and dressed casually, wearing a fitted T-shirt and jeans. When I could speak, I asked her who she was. She told me that we had met a few days earlier just outside the small town of Waterville. Her car had been stopped at the side of the road with a flat tire.

I recalled the encounter. She had tried to change the tire herself but had spilled the wheel's lug nuts down the side of the incline into a deep gorge, leaving her stranded. I had taken a nut from each of the other tires and attached her spare.

She had offered me a ride to Spokane that I turned down. Just before she drove off, she gave me her business card, which (since I'd thrown my cell phone away on the first day of my walk) was the only contact information the police found on me. They called her and, inexplicably, she came. Her name was Annie, but she told me to call her Angel. "That's what my friends call me," she said.

She was with me when the doctor told me that I would need several weeks of convalescence at home.

"I'm homeless," I said.

There was an awkward silence. Then Angel said, "He can come home with me."

Since then she had come every day to see me, staying for about an hour each night, our conversation as stilted as two teenagers on a blind date. I wasn't bothered that she came—I was lonely and appreciated the company—I just didn't know *why* she came.

Tonight's visit (angelic visitations, she called them) was later than usual. When I woke, she was looking down, reading a paperback Amish love story. As I looked at her, a song started playing in my head.

I'm on top of the world looking down on creation . . .

The tune, ironically cheerful, kept on playing, as annoyingly insistent as a scratched vinyl record. The melody was from a seventies song—something from my childhood. The *Carpenters*. My mother loved the Carpenters. She'd talk about Richard and Karen Carpenter like they were relatives.

Even as she was dying of cancer, she'd play their records. *Especially* when she was dying. She said their music kept her spirits up. As a kid, I knew the words to all their songs by heart. I still did. "Close to You," "Rainy Days and Mondays," "Hurting Each Other"; I remember tracing the Carpenters' signature logo on typing paper, then trying to improve it, which was probably my first commercial graphic attempt.

My mother would play their albums on our walnut-veneered, Zenith console stereo (a Plymouth-sized appliance which nearly took up the entire east wall of our living room), and their music would fill our home, which always made me feel peaceful because I knew it made my mother happy.

Angel was still engrossed in her book when I realized why the tune had come to mind. She *looked* like Karen Carpenter. Not exactly. She was blond and probably a little prettier, but close enough to warrant a second glance. I wondered if she could sing. As I was musing over the similarities, Angel suddenly looked up.

She smiled when she saw me looking at her. "Hi."

My mouth was parched and I ran my tongue over my lips before speaking. "Hi."

"How are you feeling?"

"A little better than yesterday. How long have you been here?"

"About an hour." Silence. Then she said, "You were talking in your sleep."

"Did I say anything profound?"

"I think you were calling for someone . . . McKay or McKale?"

I winced but offered no explanation.

"I talked to your nurse. She said that if your scan turns out well, you could leave in a few days. Maybe even Monday." Her mouth twisted a little. "Halloween. Scary."

"That would be nice," I said.

After a moment she said, "My offer's still open. You're welcome to stay with me. I've already moved some things around in my apartment . . ." then she added cautiously, "just in case."

"That's kind of you," I said without commitment.

She looked at me apprehensively. Nearly a minute had passed when she asked, "What do you think?"

What did I think? I had spent the last few days considering the few options I had. After the destruction of my life, the only friend I had left

28

was Falene, my former assistant, back in Seattle. In spite of our friendship, I couldn't go back there.

My only other option was my father in Los Angeles. If I went to California, I knew I'd never come back. And I *needed* to come back. I needed to finish my walk.

For the first time since I'd left my home, I realized that my trek was more than just a physical commitment; it was a spiritual one—like the walkabouts of the Australian aborigines or the spirit walk of the Native Americans. Something I didn't completely understand compelled me onward.

And, for whatever reason, this woman was part of my journey. There was some reason she was in my path and sitting by my bed. I just had no idea what that reason might be.

After a moment I said, "If it's not too much trouble."

Her lips rose in a slight smile and she nodded. "No trouble at all."

CHAPTER
Four

Sometimes Mother Nature has PMS.

Alan Christoffersen's diary

I suddenly realized the date—October 28—McKale's and my wedding anniversary.

Our wedding day wasn't the kind of day anyone dreams of, unless you include nightmares. Just about everything went wrong, which, I guess, is what happens when mothers aren't involved—or Mother Nature is.

We had planned a small ceremony at the Arcadia Arboretum and Botanical Gardens just a few miles from our home near the racetrack at Santa Anita Park. On the east side of the arboretum was a beautiful rose garden with a vine-covered gazebo, the back of the structure overhanging a pond filled with koi and lily pads. The setting was perfect. The weather, not so much. It started raining around 8 P.M. the evening before our wedding and didn't let up until about two hours before our ceremony. *Everything* was soggy. The lawn was as saturated as a deep-sea sponge and water ran out along its borders in rivulets and streams.

We should have rented a large tent in case of

inclement weather, but our wedding planner, Diane—McKale's cousin—was so certain of her luck (it never rains on my parties, she boasted) that she had only reserved a small, 20-by-20-foot canopy as a backup.

After the rain stopped, Diane and her helpers scurried about the yard, setting up chairs, tossing rose petals, tying ribbons, stringing up lights and setting up an array of wide, fabric umbrellas, just in case the rain started again.

As an ornamental backdrop for the gazebo, Diane hung strings of twinkling white lights and brought in two meter-high white column-style pedestals topped with large ceramic vases.

As everything took shape, the members of the string quartet assumed their places next to the gazebo and began playing Pachelbel's Canon in D.

It would seem that Mother Nature had been waiting for the optimal moment to strike, for just as the finishing touches were being made—and Diane was looking rather pleased with herself—a microburst hit. In one great sneeze, the umbrellas were turned inside out or took flight (I watched one guest chase one through the parking lot), the vases fell and shattered, and the rose petals so delicately thrown about were brusquely blown away.

The scene would have been amusing if it weren't so tragic. Our unfortunate guests ran around the garden in a state of panic, clinging to their hats, garments, or spouses. All was chaos.

As soon as the ceremony's accoutrements were sufficiently destroyed, the wind stopped, as if Mother Nature was taking a moment to survey her handiwork. Then the rain started back in earnest.

The preacher, Reverend Handy, a friend of McKale's father, had come from another wedding and gotten caught in the weather-delayed traffic, arriving on the scene just fifteen minutes before the appointed hour. I noticed his stunned expression as he surveyed the ruins of our day. The setting looked like a news clip from one of those interviews you see broadcast from a trailer park after a tornado's blown through—complete and utter devastation.

At noon I took my place under the dripping gazebo and waited for my bride, standing before a small gathering of survivors congregated beneath a bobbing sea of umbrellas.

And then she appeared, her father on one side, the distraught Diane on the other, wet and carrying an umbrella. McKale was my sun, radiant in a strapless ivory dress. As she neared, we looked into each other's eyes and the chaos melted away. I slid the ring on her finger, hoping that she hadn't seen the carnage as an omen for our marriage.

After we were pronounced man and wife, most of our guests fled while those remaining crowded under a dripping canopy to await the cutting of the cake.

McKale was quiet as we drove off on our honeymoon, the rhythm of the windshield wipers filling the gap of our silence. When we were alone in our hotel room, I said, "I'm sorry about how things turned out." I expected her to burst into tears, but she didn't. Instead she looked down at her diamond ring, then took my hand. "I would have married you with a plastic ring, standing in a landfill in the middle of a hurricane. The show was for them. All I wanted was you. It's the best day of my life."

That's when I was sure we'd last forever.

Angel was by my side when I realized that McKale's wedding ring was missing. I started frantically patting around my chest and neck. I must have looked like I was having a heart attack or stroke because Angel looked alarmed. "What is it?" she asked. "Should I call a nurse?"

"They took it," I said.

"Took *what?*"

"My wife's wedding ring. It was on a chain around my neck."

She looked almost as distraught as I felt. "I'll see if the nurses know anything about it." She pressed the call button, and within a few moments a nurse I'd never seen before appeared in the doorway.

"Do you need something?"

Angel said, "Alan's missing some jewelry."

"Well, we usually remove jewelry in the ER." She turned to me. "What are you missing?"

"It's a woman's diamond ring on a gold chain," I said.

"It's probably in your locker. I can check on it for you."

I lay my head back into the pillow. "What's your name?" I asked.

"Alice."

"Alice," I said, "do you know where the rest of my things are? I was carrying a backpack when I was attacked."

"No. But I can ask the police. They're just down the hall."

"Why are they down the hall?"

"They're standing guard over one of the men who attacked you."

I had forgotten. My doctor had told me earlier that one of the young men who had assaulted me was also in the hospital—not that I was planning to send a get-well card—but it was good information to have.

Alice said, "The police have asked to speak with you when you're feeling up to it."

"I'm up to it," I said quickly. I wanted to talk

to the police for my own reasons—I had questions about the night.

It was less than five minutes after her departure when two police officers in uniform entered my room, stopping a few feet inside my door. The officer closest to me, a short, slim man, spoke. "Mr. Christoffersen, I'm Officer Eskelson. This is my partner, Lieutenant Foulger. May we come in?"

I looked at the other officer who was standing behind him. "Yes."

Eskelson turned to Angel. "Is this your wife?"

"No," she said. "I'm just a friend."

"Do you mind if she's here for our interview?"

"I can leave," Angel said.

"She's fine," I said.

Angel remained seated. Officer Eskelson walked to the side of my bed. "How are you feeling?"

"Other than the concussion and three knife wounds?" I asked.

"I'm sorry, I'll keep this short." He lifted a pad and pen. "I'd like you to describe, in your own words, the night of your assault."

I've never understood why people said "in your own words." *Who else's words would I use?*

"It was around midnight when I stopped at the Hilton in Airway Heights for a room, but they didn't have any vacancies, so I had to go on to Spokane. I had walked about a mile when I heard some rap music and a car pulled up alongside me, a yellow Impala with a black stripe.

"There were some rough-looking kids in the car. I assumed they were gang members. They started yelling things at me. I just ignored them, but they pulled off the side of the road and got out of their car."

"Would you recognize these youths?"

"You mean like in a police lineup?"

He nodded.

"I don't know. Some of them. I thought you had them in custody."

"We do," Foulger said.

Eskelson said, "So after they pulled over, what happened?"

"They told me to give them my pack. I tried to talk them out of it. That's when the guy who stabbed me said they were going to take it after they beat me up."

"Is that what he said, 'beat you up'?"

"I think his actual words were, 'mess you up.' He said they were out looking for a 'bum to roll.'"

He scribbled on his pad. "Then what happened?"

"He came at me."

"The kid who stabbed you?"

I nodded. "I hit him and he fell over. Then one of the other guys hit me over the head with something. It felt like a pipe or a club."

"It was a baseball bat," Lieutenant Foulger said, clearing his throat. "Louisville Slugger."

"He just about knocked me out. I saw stars, but somehow I kept on my feet. Then everything got crazy. They all came at me at once. Someone knocked me to the ground and everyone was kicking me. The big guy kept stomping on my head. Then everything stopped. I looked up and the little guy took out a knife and asked me if I wanted to die."

Eskelson took his phone and showed me a picture of a young man. The picture had been taken in the hospital. "This guy?

I had to examine the image closely. The young man in the picture looked much different than the cocky, knife-wielding thug I'd encountered. Half of his face was eclipsed by gauze bandages and an oxygen tube ran down from his nose. He looked small and frail.

"That looks like him."

He scribbled on his pad. "Were those his exact words? 'Do you want to die?' "

"I'm pretty sure of it."

He wrote on his pad. "Then what?"

"I don't remember being stabbed. Someone kicked me in the face. The next thing I remember was the paramedics loading me onto a stretcher." I combed my hair back with my hand. "So tell me, why am I still alive?"

"Luck," Eskelson said, dropping his pad to his side. "Or God didn't want you dead. While you were being assaulted, a truck passing westbound saw what was happening. Fortunately for you, the truck's occupants had both the inclination and the courage to get involved."

"And shotguns," Foulger added.

"The men had been out duck hunting," Eskelson said. "They laid on their horn, then drove across the median right up to the crime scene."

Foulger jumped in. "As they got out of their truck, Marcus Franck, the kid with the knife, went at one of the men, so he shot him."

"How is he?" I asked. "The kid."

"Not good," Officer Foulger said, his lips tightening. "Twenty-gauge shotgun blast from eight, nine yards, he's a mess. He probably won't make it."

"The nurse said you're guarding him."

"He's not going anywhere," Foulger said. "We're more concerned about who might come to visit."

Officer Eskelson continued, "The hunters ordered the rest of the gang to the ground and called 911. You were bleeding pretty badly. One of the hunters administered first aid until the paramedics arrived. They saved your life."

"What are their names?" I asked.

"Since there's a potential fatality, their names

are confidential. But I can tell them that you'd like to talk to them. I've been keeping them apprised of both yours and the boy's condition."

"I understand."

"The doctor told us you'll be here for at least a few more days. After that, where can we get ahold of you?" Eskelson asked.

"My place," Angel said. "He's going to be staying with me until he's recovered." She gave them her phone number.

Eskelson said to Angel, "You look familiar."

"I'm a dispatcher for the Spokane Police Department."

"I thought I knew you," Foulger said.

"The nurse said you might know where my backpack is," I said.

"It's at the station. We can bring it by later tonight."

"Thank you. Will you let me know how the boy does?"

"No problem. At least one of us will be here for the next day or two. If you need something or remember anything else relevant to the assault, just call."

"Get well," Foulger said.

"Thank you."

After they left, Angel walked up to the side of the bed, placing her hands on the railing. "You okay?"

"Yes. So you're with the police?"

"Not really. I'm a dispatcher."

"Were you on call when I was attacked?"

"No. That was someone from the night shift." She patted my arm. "I better go. It's late. But tomorrow's Saturday, so I'll be back in the morning." She started to walk away, then stopped and turned back. "I didn't know the whole story. You know, it's a miracle you're still alive."

I carefully rubbed my hand over my abdomen. "I suppose so."

"Makes you think," she said thoughtfully. "Good night." She walked out of the room.

CHAPTER
Five

I tried to walk today. I felt as awkward
as a baby taking his first steps and I
probably looked about the same.

Alan Christoffersen's diary

Sometime in the night the police returned my
backpack. I woke to see it propped up in the
corner of the room. I had the nurse on call look
through it and retrieve my diary and a pen.

Angel arrived a few hours later. She was
dressed in an exercise outfit. Her hair was pulled
back and, in the morning light, I noticed for the
first time the deep, ragged scars that ran across
her hairline and down the right side of her face
to her jaw. I wondered how I'd never noticed
them before.

"Good morning," she said. "How are you
feeling?"

"A little better. They might get me up to walk
today."

"Big day." She looked curiously at the leather
book lying by my side. "What's that?"

"My journal. I've decided to chronicle my
journey."

"Really? Am I in there?"

"Of course."

"I wish that I had kept a journal," she said. "In high school I had a friend who kept one. She used to write lies in it."

"She'd lie in her journal?"

"She said that when she was old and couldn't remember anything she could read her journal and think she had a great life."

I grinned. "There's a certain logic to that."

"I suppose."

"I used to write copy for an advertising agency. So I guess I'm not so different from your friend."

This interested her. "Really? I've always wanted to be a writer."

"What kind?"

"I want to write screenplays. I've actually started one."

"What's it about?"

"It's still rough, but it's about a woman who is betrayed by her husband and friends, so she fakes her own death and takes on a new identity."

"That sounds intriguing."

"I have the first half finished. I just can't come up with a good beginning. Something catchy, you know?"

"I'm an expert at catchy. That's the domain of the ad guy—thirty seconds to own you. How about something like this—'Even though the police dug in my backyard all afternoon, they didn't find a single body.'"

She laughed. "That's compelling. But what if my character doesn't have any bodies in the backyard?"

"Everyone has bodies," I said.

I noticed a slight twinge.

A half hour later Norma came into the room holding a long white strap with a silver buckle. "Well, Mr. Alan, I have good news and good news. Which do you want first?"

"Surprise me."

"First, I heard you were looking for this." She handed me the chain with McKale's ring.

I eagerly reached for it. "Thank you."

As I strung the chain around my neck, she said, "The other good news is—you passed your CT scan."

"Do I get a diploma for that?"

"You get something better. You get to walk." Then she added, "If you can."

"What do you mean, *if*? I've walked more than three hundred miles in the last two weeks."

Norma rested her hands on her hips. "Considering your wounds, it might not be as easy as you think. What you went through is like having a couple nasty C-sections. So let's make your first goal something attainable, like to the bathroom."

"Followed by a victory lap around the hospital," I said.

43

"We'll see." She laid the long white strap on my bed.

"What's that?" I asked.

"It's a gait belt. In case you fall."

I grinned at the idea of her holding me up, as she was half my size. "You're going to keep me from falling?"

"I'm stronger than you think. So, can you sit up?"

I thought it a funny question. "Of course." I pushed my elbows down on the bed and lifted my chest. Pain shot up through my abdomen, taking my breath away. I blanched. "Oh."

Norma looked at me knowingly, as if she was restraining an "I told you so."

"That hurt a bit more than I thought it would," I said.

Norma asked, "Can you swing your legs over the side of the bed?"

As I shifted my body, I realized just how dependent my legs were on my stomach muscles. Walking wasn't going to be as easy as I thought. In one fateful night my goal had changed from Key West to the bathroom door. It took me a couple of minutes before I could dangle my legs over the side.

"Good. Now hold there for a moment." Norma got some slippers from my closet and brought them over. She knelt down and put them on my feet, clamped off my catheter, then stood. She put the gait belt around my waist and fastened it. "Are you ready?"

I nodded. "Yeah."

"Now slowly slide forward, putting your weight on the balls of your feet."

I pushed myself closer to the side of the bed, pulling my hospital gown down over my thighs. When my feet touched the floor, I began to lean forward. Incredible pain shot through my body, like jolts of electricity. "Ah." I took another deep breath. I was truly surprised by the intensity of the pain. The bathroom now looked a mile away.

"Not ready for the victory lap yet?" Norma said.

I took a deep breath. "That . . . hurts."

"Do you want to continue?"

"Yes."

"We'll try just a few steps this morning. Baby steps." She looked at Angel. "Can you give me a hand?"

Angel stood. "What do you want me to do?"

"Let him lean on your shoulder a little." She turned to me. "We're going to help you stand."

Both of them put a hand behind me as I put my arms around their shoulders. "Ready?"

"Yes."

"Let's go."

I slid to the edge of the bed. My eyes watered with the pain and I lightly groaned.

"Just take it easy," Norma said. "We're in no hurry."

"I am," I said. I clenched my jaw, then leaned forward until I was standing. They both took their hands away from me but remained close.

"How do you feel?" Norma asked.

"Like I've been cut in two and taped back together."

"That's a fairly accurate description."

I took a small step with my right foot—actually more of a shuffle than a step, maybe 6 inches. I paused, then moved my left foot up to my right foot. *This is bad,* I thought.

"That's good," Norma said. "You did it. Now try another."

I shuffled forward again, feeling like an old man. I was halfway to the bathroom when I began to wonder how I was going to make it back to the bed. "I think I better go back."

"Let's try turning around," Norma said.

I shuffled in a circle until I was facing the bed. Three days ago I was measuring my walks in miles. Now I was counting steps. Eighteen of them and I was exhausted. I walked back to the bed, turned around, leaned against the side of the bed then lay back. Mercifully, Norma lifted my legs onto the mattress.

"You did great," Norma said. "That was a great start."

"There was nothing great about that," I said.

"Sure there was," she replied. "You're just more damaged than you thought."

Up until that moment I had been in a state of denial, telling myself that in spite of my doctor's warning, I was going to grab my backpack and walk out of the hospital. The reality was, I was going to have to go through an extended period of recovery. The thought painfully reminded me of McKale's weeks of hospital rehabilitation after her accident.

"I know it doesn't seem like much, but your stomach muscles were severed. It's going to take a while before you're back at it."

At that moment I was filled with anger at everything that had grounded me: my body, the Hilton that had no vacancies, the gang, and especially the kid with the knife who was somewhere on my floor of the hospital. Languishing in a hospital bed wasn't part of my plan. *Hadn't I already suffered enough?*

To make matters worse, the seasons had already been stacked against me. I had planned to cross through the Idaho panhandle, then Montana and Wyoming, and with some luck, make it out of the mountains before the heaviest snows hit and closed the highways. That hope was gone. By the time I was walking again, the roads would be impassable. Like it or not, I was grounded until spring.

• • •

After Norma left the room, Angel sat down again, scooting her chair closer to me. "Are you okay?"

"What do you think?" I snapped. "Walking was the only thing I had. Now I'm going to be stuck in this godforsaken place until spring."

She looked at me, her face showing hurt. "I'm sorry."

I looked at her and sighed. "No, *I'm* sorry. It's not your fault. I'm just upset."

After a few minutes of silence she said, "Maybe I'll go do my grocery shopping. Do you need anything from the store?"

I couldn't believe how kind she was being after I'd just yelled at her. "Pop-Tarts," I said.

"Pop-Tarts?"

"Strawberry Pop-Tarts."

"Pop-Tarts it is. I'll bring some tonight."

"You're coming back tonight?"

"If it's okay with you."

"I don't know why you'd want to."

"I like seeing you," she said. "Do you play cards?"

"Texas Hold 'em, Hearts, and Gin Rummy."

"I'll bring some cards." She stood. "See you tonight."

"Angel, I really am sorry."

"Don't worry about it. I'd do the same thing." She touched my arm, then walked out the door.

After Angel left, I lay back in my bed, thinking about her. She really was kind.

Later that afternoon Norma came back in. "I brought you something," she said, holding up a piece of paper.

Affectus, qui passio est, desinit esse passio simulatque eius claram et distinctam formamus ideam.

I looked at the sign without comprehension. "I don't read Latin."

"Actually, neither do I. It's from the philosopher Spinoza. It says, and I'm paraphrasing here, 'Suffering ceases to be suffering as soon as we form a clear picture of it.' My father gave me this a few years back when I had a stillborn baby. It's helped me to get through it. I know you're in a lot of pain and you're frustrated. But this will pass and before you know it you'll be walking again. I promise."

I looked at the paper. "Would you mind hanging it up?"

"I'd be glad to. I'll go find some tape." She left the room.

Suffering ceases to be suffering when we form a clear picture of it. I wondered if that was the reason I felt so compelled to write in my journal.

When she came back, she taped the sign on my closet door. "How's that?"

"Perfect."

"Ready to walk again?"

"Sure."

I clenched my teeth as I moved my feet to the side of the bed, then slid forward. The pain felt worse this time. Norma fastened the gait belt around my waist.

"Okay, take it easy. One step at a time."

I took in a deep breath, then took a step, met with searing pain. I paused, then took another. The same. I took a third, then stopped. "I can't do it."

"You're still sore from this morning," she said softly. She put my arm around her shoulder and slowly helped me back. I sat back and she lifted my feet onto the bed. "We'll try again tomorrow."

I closed my eyes and sighed.

"Hey, you'll get this. Before you know it, you'll be running marathons." She patted my leg. "My shift is over. I'll see you tomorrow."

After she left, I tried to form a clear picture of my suffering. It didn't make the pain go away.

Angel returned around seven. She was wearing a long navy blue wool coat and was carrying a plastic grocery sack from which she brought out two boxes of Pop-Tarts. "I got your Pop-Tarts," she said. "I didn't know if you wanted the

50

frosted kind or plain, so I got you both." She set the boxes on the table next to my bed.

"Thank you." I opened the box with the frosted pastries and took out a package, opening the wrapper with my teeth. I handed a Pop-Tart to Angel. "Want one?"

"Sure." She took the pastry. Then, as she walked to the other side of my bed, she noticed the quote Norma had taped to the closet door. "What's this?"

"It's something Norma brought in."

She squinted as she read it. "Emotion, which is suffering, stops . . . no . . . ceases to be suffering when a clear and distinct idea is formed."

"You read Latin?" I asked.

"Almost," she said. "I had classes in high school." I noticed that she made no comment as to the message or its meaning. She took her coat off.

"Your family must wonder why you've been gone so much lately," I said.

"There's no family," she said. "Just me."

"Well, then your friends must wonder what you're up to."

A sardonic grin crossed her face. "No one's filing a missing person report, if that's what you mean. I'm kind of a loner."

I looked at her quizzically. "I never would have pegged you for a loner."

"Why is that?"

"You're a very friendly, kind person. It doesn't add up."

51

"I could say the same about you."

"Things happen."

"Exactly," she replied. "Things happen." She looked at me for a moment. "I was thinking about the ring you were looking for. Did you lose your wife?"

"Yeah."

"I'm sorry."

"Me too."

She put her hand on my arm. "I know this is a dumb question, but is there anything I can do?"

"I wish there were." After a moment I asked, "Have you ever been married?"

She hesitated. "No."

"Are you from Spokane?"

"I was born here. But my family moved to Minnesota when I was eight. I got a job offer a few months ago and decided to move back."

"So what's it like being a police dispatcher?"

She shrugged. "It's not dull, but it's depressing. Seems all day long I witness the worst of mankind."

"I never thought of that. Where in Minnesota are you from?"

"Near Lake Minnetonka in Wayzata."

"I've never been to Minnesota. I hear it's beautiful."

"It's cold," she said shortly. "Very cold."

From her expression I guessed that she wasn't just talking about the weather.

CHAPTER
Six

In college I took a social psychology
course, something I thought useful for
a career in advertising. Psychologists
tested the story of the Good Samaritan.
What they learned gives us reason to
pause. The greatest determinant of
who stopped to help the stranger in
need was not compassion, morality,
or religious creed. It was those who
had the time. Makes me wonder if I
have time to do good.
Apparently, Angel does.

Alan Christoffersen's diary

Early the next morning I was reading the newspaper when Norma walked into my room with
her chart. I was testing my legs as I read, lifting
one at a time and holding it for as long as I
could, which, pitifully, could be measured in
microseconds.

"Hi," she said. She looked a little stressed.

I set down the paper. "How are you today?" I
asked.

"Fine. The $100,000 question is, how are you?"

"Still here."

"Did you hear . . . ?" she hesitated. "The boy died."

"Who?"

"The boy who stabbed you."

I shook my head. "No." I wasn't sure how to respond. I wasn't even sure what to feel. Revenge, justice, pity, sadness? The truth is, I didn't feel anything.

After a moment she said, "The doctor will be in to see you this afternoon."

"Will she tell me when I can go?"

"I think so." She checked one of my monitors, then asked, "Are you ready to try to walk again?"

"Sure," I said.

"I've got a few other patients I need to see, then I'll be back." She walked out.

I lay back and sighed. I wasn't feeling any better than I was before.

A half hour after breakfast Norma walked back into my room holding the gait belt. "Let's do this."

She clamped off my catheter, then I sat up and swung my legs over the side of the bed a little too quickly. I clenched my teeth with pain.

"Just a moment," Norma said. "Before you try again, I want to ask you something."

I looked at her expectantly. "Yes?"

"Why do you want to walk? What's your number-one reason?"

"So I can take out this"—I restrained from swearing—"catheter."

She looked at me thoughtfully. "Angel told me that you're walking to Key West. Is that true?"

"I was trying."

"There's got to be a story there."

I looked down for a moment. Then I said, "In the last month I've lost my wife, my home, and my business."

Her expression changed. "I'm so sorry, I didn't know." She gently touched my arm. "So that's why you're walking."

"Walking is what's been keeping me going. Without Key West, I have nothing."

She nodded slowly. "Don't forget that. Now let's walk."

I again set my feet on the floor and began to shift my weight. Actually, the pain wasn't as severe as it had been the day before. "I'm ready," I said.

Norma grabbed my arm as I forced myself to my feet, bracing against the pain. I took a step forward. Pain again seared through my body, but somehow it lacked the severity of before. *I can handle that,* I thought. I took another step, paused, then took another. "I can do this," I said.

"I know you can," Norma said.

I took six more steps, then stopped. Either the pain had relaxed or my determination had grown sufficient to match it. I took a few more steps, then reached out and grabbed the bathroom's handle.

Norma smiled. "You did it."

I took a deep breath. "Now, let's see if I can make it back." I slowly turned around, then, without pausing, walked to the bed. Norma clapped.

When I was lying comfortably in bed, I asked, "Would you take my catheter out now?"

"Gladly." She shut my door, then put on latex gloves, pulled aside my gown, and removed my catheter.

"Finally," I said.

"You earned it."

As she was taking off her gloves, I said to her, "How did you know to ask me why I wanted to walk?"

"It's my experience that if you focus on the why, the *how* takes care of itself." She walked over and touched me on the arm. "I'm proud of you. I knew you could do it. I'll check on you again before my shift ends." She started to the door.

"Norma?"

She turned back. "Yes?"

"Thank you."

She smiled and walked out.

I spent the rest of the morning reading. Norma came back in around two with a stack of color copies. "I brought you something." She handed me the papers.

I shuffled through pictures of beaches and ocean. "What are these?"

"Pictures of Key West. I printed them off of the Internet."

"I mean, what are they for?"

"Reminders," she said. "I'll hang them up if you like."

I handed them back to her. "Sure."

"Good. Are you ready to go for another walk?"

"Yes. To the bathroom, please."

I put my hands on the edge of the bed and pushed myself up. I walked to the bathroom in about the same time as before, went inside and locked the door, and used the toilet. I came out a few minutes later. "I feel human again."

"One small step for man, one giant leap for dignity."

I smiled as I slowly walked back. When I reached my bed, she said, "That's awesome, Alan. Well done."

"Thanks, coach." I sat back on the bed.

She lifted the Key West pictures from the nightstand. "I'll hang these for you."

There were six pictures in all. She began hanging them on the wall in front of my bed.

"So do you have big plans for tonight?" I asked.

"My husband has to work late, so I'm going

to my mother's to help her clean out her basement. She's been on this cleaning kick lately."

"Sounds fun. Wish I could help."

"I bet you do," she said sardonically. "How about you? Any exciting plans? Skateboarding? Tennis?"

"I thought I'd just hang out here."

She smiled. "Good idea. Is your friend coming today?"

"You mean Angel?"

She nodded.

"I think so. She didn't say."

"I had a good talk with her yesterday. She's really quite interesting. How long have you known her?"

"Actually, I don't."

She finished taping the last picture and turned back. "What do you mean?"

"I met her just a little over a week ago."

"That's funny. She talks about you as if you were her best friend. You know, she did something really surprising. I was admiring her sapphire necklace and she took it off and gave it to me. I'm sure it was worth at least a thousand dollars."

"She gave you a sapphire necklace?"

"Well, she tried to. I didn't accept it."

I wasn't sure what to think of that. "She's a bit of a mystery. I can't figure out why she's been so good to me."

"Maybe she's one of those rare people who sincerely cares about others. Or maybe she's an angel."

"An angel?"

"Well, that's her name, isn't it?" she said, patting my arm. "Dr. McDonald will be in to see you before her shift is over, so in case she releases you, don't go running out of here without saying goodbye."

"I don't think I'll be running anywhere. Have fun at your mother's."

She grinned. "You know I will. Take care. And good job today. You're my hero."

After she walked out, I thought about our conversation about Angel. I didn't mean to question her motives—or maybe I did—but I didn't really know what was driving her. Maybe she was, as Norma speculated, just altruistic—a modern-day saint. I knew people like that, not many, but a few. My mother was like that. So was my former assistant Falene, who for no apparent reason had stood with me through all the chaos and crisis I had gone through. In spite of the horrors we read about in the papers, there are still people out there with selfless, giving hearts.

But my mother was my mother and Falene knew me. Angel was a complete stranger. Something didn't fit.

Dr. McDonald didn't come in to see me until

after five. As she entered, she glanced at the pictures on my wall. "Looks like Key West has come to you." She walked to the side of my bed. "Sorry I'm so late. I had a patient whose heart decided to take a holiday. I hear you're walking again."

"More like shuffling, but I made it to the bathroom."

"Excellent. Your CT scans show no further damage, the rest of your vitals have been consistently stable, and you seem to be recovering without any complications, so I'd like to keep you here for another twenty-four hours, then you're free to go."

"Fair enough."

"I've written out a prescription for an antibiotic and a week's worth of oral morphine tablets to help with the pain. The dosage is 10 milligrams, and you'll be taking them for comfort measures, so you can quit taking them whenever you feel up to it. We're going to send you home in your bandages and have you check back with us next week to remove your stitches. I'll leave your prescriptions here." She set the papers on my bedside table. "So the word on the floor is you're walking to Key West."

"That's my plan."

"Hopefully you won't have any more detours." She smiled. "Good luck, Mr. Christoffersen."

···

Angel arrived about ten minutes after the doctor left. Her eyes were red, as if she'd been crying. "How's your day been?" she asked.

"Not bad," I said. "How was yours?"

"I'm okay," she said. She sat down.

"I walked on my own," I said.

"And I missed it?" She sounded disappointed, like a parent who had missed her toddler's first steps.

"It's not a big deal," I said. "The doctor was just here. She said I could leave tomorrow."

This clearly pleased her. "Good. Everything's ready at home. Is there anything else you need?"

"I need my prescriptions filled," I said, pointing to the table.

She stood and lifted the papers. "No problem."

"My wallet is in the small zipper outside of my backpack. There's a credit card inside."

"Okay," she said. "I'll take care of them right now."

I noticed she left without taking my card.

CHAPTER
Seven

There are people who come into our lives as welcome as a cool breeze in summer—and last about as long.

Alan Christoffersen's diary

The next day Norma was fussing around in my room while we waited for Angel to arrive. Angel had planned to get off work a little early. She arrived at quarter of six and was out of breath. "Sorry I'm late," she panted. "I was having BG problems."

"BG?" I said.

"Blood glucose," Norma said. "Are you diabetic?"

"Type one. I was a little low this afternoon."

"You don't live alone, do you?" Norma asked.

"Yes."

Norma cocked her head. "That's really dangerous. Now I'm especially glad that Alan will be staying with you."

"So am I," Angel said. She held up a paper sack. "And I got your prescriptions filled." She unzipped my pack and stuffed the medications inside.

"I just need to get dressed," I said.

"We'll give you some privacy," Norma said.

A couple minutes later Norma knocked, then opened my door. "Ready?" She entered pushing a wheelchair. Angel was behind her.

"Would you like to take Key West with you?" Norma asked, taking down the pictures.

I turned to Angel. "Will there be wall space?"

"Plenty."

"Okay. I'll take Key West."

"I'll get the car," Angel said. She lifted my backpack, though not without difficulty. "I'll meet you downstairs." She walked out.

I stood up, walked to the wheelchair, and sat down.

"You know, I'm going to miss you," I said to Norma.

"I'll miss you too. Will you send me a card when you get to Key West?"

"Ycs."

Norma wheeled me out to the elevator and pushed the button for the lobby. A moment later I was outside the hospital.

I recognized Angel's car from our first encounter —an aged, silver-gray Chevrolet Malibu which she pulled up to the loading zone right in front of us. She put the car in park, climbed out, and walked around, opening the passenger side door.

Stepping over the curb suddenly looked daunting. "I can do this," I said, though less certain than hopeful. I slowly stood, pushing myself up from the armrests. I couldn't believe how much it still hurt to move. Getting back into shape wasn't going to happen overnight. I stood for a moment, testing my balance.

"Got it?" Norma asked.

"I'm fine."

"Good luck," she said.

"Thank you. For everything."

She leaned forward and we hugged. Then I carefully stepped off the curb into the car. I lifted my feet inside. Angel leaned over me and clicked my seat belt, then shut the car door.

Norma waved, then grasped the handles of the wheelchair and pushed it back inside. Angel climbed into her seat and started the car. "Norma was great."

"Yes she was," I said.

"Now it's my turn to take care of you." She put the car in drive and we headed for her home.

CHAPTER
Eight

I feel like a kite caught in a hurricane.

Alan Christoffersen's diary

Angel lived fifteen minutes from the hospital in a small suburb east of the city. We drove over some train tracks and I held my abdomen and grimaced. Angel glanced over at me. "I'm sorry," she said. "We're almost there."

As we drove, the landscape of the city flashed by me like a dull cinema. All I could think was how much I didn't want to be in Spokane. The city looked as gray to me as the weather, though it was likely more a reflection of my grayness inside. I had been to Spokane before, twice, and enjoyed my stay, but this time the city seemed unwelcoming.

Spokane is the second-largest city in Washington, and a lot like Seattle except without the population, the business community, the economy, the waterfront, the politics, the coffee . . . actually, Spokane is nothing at all like Seattle.

I'm sure the people who live here are just as warm, intelligent, and cultured as those in Seattle, maybe more so, and, in their defense, they didn't give the world grunge music nor Sir Mix-a-lot. It's just different. A lot different.

As I said, my problem wasn't with Spokane as a locale, it was with my being *stuck* there. I was still running from Seattle, and my legs had been taken out from under me just a few miles from the Washington-Idaho border. I wanted out of the state more than I could say.

Angel's apartment was located in an old, A-framed home just a few miles north of Gonzaga University on a pine-lined street called Nora. The house, which had been divided into three apartments, was shingled, with a steeply pitched roof and peeling yellow paint that made the home stand out, not just because of its color, but because most of the other homes on the street were constructed of brick. The windows were oddly narrow and irregular, some taller than others. There was a good-sized front yard, and overgrown holly bushes surrounded the house's exterior.

The neighborhood seemed staid for a university area, which meant the surrounding homes were either occupied by students who were serious about their studies or hungover from all-night partying. I was hoping for the former.

About half of the houses were decorated for Halloween, some elaborately with giant spider webs and other haunts. The sum of the decorations at Angel's place was a dried cornstalk on the ground next to the front door.

Angel pulled her car up to the curb in front of her home and killed the engine. "Here we are. I'll get the door for you." She walked around to my side and opened my door.

Painfully, I pivoted my body so I was facing out, but this was the extent of my acrobatics. I looked up at her. "Can you give me a hand?"

"Of course. On the count of three I'll pull," she said.

"Okay," I said, planting my feet on the asphalt road.

"One, two, three . . ." she pulled back as I leaned forward and stood up. Crippling pain shot up my body, taking away my breath.

"Just a minute," I said.

"Are you all right?"

"I'll be okay." When the pain eased, I said, "All right. Next."

She came to my side and took my arm. "Let's go." I stepped up over the curb onto the yellowed lawn. I paused and looked up and down the sidewalk. Eventually, I would be walking these sidewalks, but for the moment just making it to the house and up the front stairs seemed a formidable goal.

I shuffled up a concrete walkway to the stairs that led up to Angel's apartment. The stairs were narrow and steep, poured from concrete with a wrought-iron railing that seeped rust into the cement. I clutched the railing and looked skeptically at the first step.

"Are you ready for this?" she asked.

"It's walk or crawl."

"Let me help you. Put your arm around my shoulder."

I put my right arm over her shoulder and gripped the railing with my left hand. I took a deep breath. "Let's go."

With her help I made it to the landing, every step accentuated with words of encouragement.

"You're doing great," she said. "Really great."

I think by *great* she meant I didn't fall.

Angel's apartment was on the main floor and situated the furthest back. She took her key out of her purse, unlocked the door, then pushed it open. "Be it ever so humble," she said.

The first thing I noticed was the smell of cooking—though I wondered how that was possible since she'd been at work all day. "Something smells good."

"Dinner's in the Crock-Pot," she replied.

The front room was larger than I expected, with a large picture window looking out over the back yard. There was a couch and a rectangular coffee table in front of a television, which was nestled into a wood-veneer cabinet. The room was uncluttered and austere, with just the barest of necessities.

There was something different about the room —something was missing—but I couldn't figure out what it was.

At the end of the hall was a small kitchen, with a tiny, Formica-topped table. The kitchen was messy.

In the hallway between the living room and the kitchen were three doors. "This is your room," she said, pushing open the south door and stepping inside. I followed her in. A queen-sized poster bed was pressed up against the corner, touching two walls and leaving a three-foot margin on the front and side. There was a small clothes closet and a chest of drawers.

"I hope it's okay."

"It's more than okay," I said.

"After dinner we can hang your pictures of Key West." She stepped back into the hallway. "My room is right here, across the hall. Just make yourself at home. I'm making a special dinner to celebrate your release from the hospital. I hope you like Italian."

"I love Italian."

"I'm making chicken cacciatore with roasted vegetable-stuffed ravioli."

"So you're a cook."

"I love to cook," she said. "But I hardly ever do it since it's just me. I need about a half hour to finish. Would you like to read something or watch TV?"

"Something mindless."

"TV it is. Let me find the remote."

I shuffled into the front room and sat down on the sofa, which was lower and softer than I expected and I fell back into the cushions like they were quicksand. I knew I wouldn't be getting up without help.

Angel found the remote on the floor next to the television and brought it to me. "I need to get your pack from the car." She went out the front door, leaving it slightly ajar, and returned a few minutes later carrying my pack over her shoulder. She was huffing a little. "I'll just put it in your room."

"*Grazie.*"

"Don't mention it." She set the pack in my room, then disappeared into the kitchen. I scanned through the programs, ending up in the middle of a public television broadcast of *Spartacus*.

About forty-five minutes later Angel came out to get me. "Dinner's ready," she said. She helped me up from the couch. When I came into the kitchen, the table was set with porcelain dinnerware and there was a flickering, slender white candle in the middle of the table.

"You went to a lot of trouble," I said.

70

"No trouble, it's a celebration."

She pulled out my chair and I slowly sat. Then she sat down across from me.

"*Buon appetito*," she said.

"You too," I replied. "Can you eat pasta with diabetes?"

"The carbs are a killer, I just don't eat as much." She lifted a small cylindrical object. "And of course I shoot up."

The meal was one of the best I'd had since I had left Seattle, and I told her so. Angel seemed very happy to see me so pleased.

"It's a pleasure cooking for someone who appreciates it."

"So, outside of work and caring for the infirm, what do you do for fun?"

"Fun?" she repeated, as if she hadn't heard the word for a while. "Well, I haven't had a lot of free time lately, but I've been watching the American Film Institute's list of the hundred greatest movies. I started with one hundred and I'm working my way up to number one."

"Which is . . .?"

"*Citizen Kane.*"

I nodded. "Orson Welles. Of course."

"Last night I watched number seventy-eight, *Rocky*. Tonight is seventy-seven, if you'd like to join me."

"I'm pretty sure I'm free. What's seventy-seven?"

"*American Graffiti.*"

"It's been at least twenty years since I saw that."

"It's a classic," she said. "Of course, you could say that about everything on the list."

Angel ate slowly, controlling how much she ate while watching me do the opposite. She seemed amused by my appetite. When I finally laid down my fork, she asked, "Can I get you anything else? A side of beef?"

I laughed out loud. "No, I think I'm about done."

She grinned. "Why don't you go back to the living room. I'll do the dishes, then I'll be in."

"I can help," I said.

"You should stay off your feet. Besides, it will only take me five minutes."

"I want to pull my weight around here."

"I'll make you a deal. As soon as you can walk around the block, I'll work you into the ground."

"That's incentive," I said.

"I'm a great motivator of men," she replied.

I was able to get myself up, though I did have to push up from the table. While she did the dishes, I went to my room. My bandages were itching a little and I pulled one of them off to inspect my wound. It was a little red around the stitches but didn't look infected. Just then I heard children's voices.

"Trick or treat!"

I leaned my head out my door. "Sounds like you have visitors." Surprisingly, Angel didn't answer the door.

I replaced my bandage then shuffled out to the couch. A few minutes later Angel walked into the front room with a bowl of miniature candy bars. She quickly opened the apartment door, set the bowl on the floor and then shut the door again.

"You know what's going to happen, don't you?" I said.

"What?"

"Some kid's going to take the whole bowl."

"Have a little faith," she said, walking back to the kitchen.

"I have faith," I replied. "That's what I would have done."

"I'm just about finished," she said, ignoring my comment. "I just need to pop some corn. You can't properly watch a movie without popcorn."

A few minutes later she came out with a sack of microwave popcorn. She inserted a disk into her DVD player. "If I had been thinking ahead, I would have rented number eighteen for tonight."

"What's eighteen?"

"Alfred Hitchcock. *Psycho*." She switched off the floor lamp, grabbed one of the pillows from the couch, then lay down across the floor in front of the sofa.

"You're sitting down there?"

"I like sitting on the floor. Feel free to own the couch."

I lay on my side and hit the button to start the movie.

It was past eleven when the movie ended. Angel stood up and turned on the lights. "That was good."

"I forgot that Richard Dreyfuss was in that," I said, "a very young Richard Dreyfuss."

"And Suzanne Somers and Cindy Williams. That movie launched a dozen sitcoms."

"What's next on the list?" I asked.

"It's supposed to be *City Lights*."

"I've never heard of it."

"It's an old Charlie Chaplin movie."

"A Charlie Chaplin film," I said, happy that one of his movies was on the list.

"It's considered one of the last great silent films. And let me tell you, it wasn't easy to find. I ordered it online, but it hasn't come yet." She went to her front door and opened it, stooping over to pick up the candy bowl. There was still candy inside. "You were wrong. There is hope for the next generation. Have a Milky Way." She threw me a miniature candy bar.

"This is the ultimate spin," I said.

"What is?"

"They cut the bar to a fraction of its size then

call it 'fun-size.' There's nothing fun at all about a smaller candy bar. It's all in the spin."

"Just like life," she said.

I nodded. "Just like life."

She walked back to me. "I'll help you up." She took both of my hands, leaning back to pull me up from the couch.

I groaned as I stood. "Getting up is always the hard part."

"Can I get you anything before bed?"

"No. I'm good. So what are you going to do when you finish watching the one hundred movies?"

She looked at me with a strange expression. "Then I'll be done." The way she said it struck me as peculiar.

She smiled. "I'll probably be gone to work by the time you get up, so I'll just leave breakfast ready for you. Don't forget to take your pain pills with food, and I'll put the Saran Wrap in the bathroom."

"Saran Wrap?"

"Remember, you're not supposed to get your bandages wet. Norma said no baths for at least a week, and when you shower you should cover your bandages with cellophane."

I nodded, impressed that she had remembered.

"She said it works best to just wrap the Saran around your body a couple times. It's not a big deal if your bandages get a little damp."

"You're a very good nurse."

"I do my best."

I shuffled toward my room with Angel by my side. When I got to my door, I turned to her. "Thanks for everything. You're more than a good nurse, you're a good person."

She looked into my eyes with a light I could not read. "I wish that were true," she said, then disappeared into her room.

CHAPTER
Nine

Today I made it to the front walk.
I don't know if I should be happy
for my achievement or depressed
that I consider it one.

Alan Christoffersen's diary

Angel was gone by the time I woke the next morning. She left a note for me on the kitchen table.

> **Breakfast in oven to warm. OJ in fridge. Please turn off oven. I'll be home around five.**
> **Have a good day, Angel** ☺

I walked over to the oven and, with some effort, leaned over and opened the door. Inside was a square pan with what looked like a baked omelet —a frittata, I guess it would be called. She didn't need to go to so much trouble, since I'd be just as happy with a bowl of Wheaties.

I turned off the oven, grabbed the pot holder she'd left on the counter, and brought out the pan. She had already set the table for me, and I dished the frittata onto my plate and placed the pan on top of the oven. I got my pain meds and orange juice (which she'd poured into a glass) and then sat down to eat. The egg-thing was delicious.

After breakfast I went into the bathroom to shower. A box of Saran Wrap sat next to the sink. I took off my clothes, wrapped the cellophane around my torso twice, then turned on the water.

I felt the water for temperature, then stepped into the tub and let the water wash over me. It was the first shower I'd had in days, and I closed my eyes, and let the warm water cover my body. I stood there for minutes.

Drying myself off wasn't easy, and it took me nearly fifteen minutes to get my clothes on. I had already discovered that tying my shoes was nearly impossible, so I loosened the laces, then dropped them on the floor and slipped my feet into them. When I was finally dressed, I walked to the front door. I didn't have a key to the apartment, so I checked to make sure that the apartment door wasn't locked, then slowly walked to the building's front door and opened it to the world outside. The street was quiet, garnished with a few smashed pumpkins.

I had planned my rehabilitation as I lay in bed the night before. My first *major* goal was to make it around the block before the snow fell, which sounds ridiculously simple, but at that time seemed as daunting to me as scaling Mt. Everest.

My first *minor* goal was making it up and down the front stair by myself, and my second was to make it all the way down the walk. If I hadn't been in such pain, I would have laughed at the absurdity of my new expectations. Just weeks ago I made a goal to walk across the country. Today I would be thrilled to make it to the sidewalk.

I grabbed onto the landing's cold wrought-iron railing and took my first step down with my right foot, then moved my left foot to the same stair. Step. Repeat. Step. Repeat. Six steps. Unless they're OCD, most people don't count steps; they just bound up and down them as quickly as they can, but to me they'd become milestones.

I was slow, but I made it to the bottom step with a minimal amount of pain. I was feeling pretty good, so I decided to press on, hobbling down the front walk toward the street. When I reached the sidewalk, I surveyed the neighborhood. Angel's building was in the middle of the block, and the sidewalk went about four homes either way before a corner.

I felt pleased with my accomplishment. I had already achieved my first goal. I also liked being outside again. The trees had lost most of their leaves, and the air was brisk and portending the changing weather.

The next week I would walk to the end of the street, and by the 14th, I would attempt to walk

79

around the block—unless it snowed. Then it would be too dangerous. I couldn't afford to fall.

I turned around in a gradual process of steps, and for about five minutes I stood there looking at the house I now lived in. It was a far cry from the $2 million behemoth I'd been thrown out of, but I was grateful for it and Angel's generosity. I wondered how long I would be here. I took a deep breath and then slowly walked back.

Climbing the stairs was much more difficult than my descent, and when I reached the landing, I stopped and let the pain wash over me.

As I stood there, one of the other apartment's tenants, a young woman with long brown hair and a backpack flung over one shoulder, walked past me without a word but smiling as she went. I walked into the house and then the apartment and went back to my bed to rest.

Angel arrived home a little before five. Something was different about her. She seemed distressed.

"How was your day?" I asked.

She shook her head. "A family of four was hit by a drunk driver. Everyone was killed except the father, who's in intensive care battling for his life, and the drunk driver, who, of course, walked away unscathed. Actually, he *ran* away unscathed. He fled the scene on foot." She looked at me with gray eyes. "Why is it that the guilty survive while the innocent die?"

Sometimes it did seem that way. "I don't know."

"*If* there is a God," she said, "He has a foul sense of irony."

I had had nearly the same thought as I looked in the mirror the day of my wife's funeral, but I was surprised to hear it coming from her. I guess I didn't expect someone named Angel to diss God.

"I'm making meatloaf for dinner," she said, turning from me. "I just need to put it in the oven."

"Are we on for a movie tonight?"

"I don't know," she said.

She clearly didn't want to talk, so while she made dinner, I went to my room and read. A half hour later she called and we sat together at the table. We ate a while without conversation. Suddenly, she asked, "How long do you think you'll be here?"

I looked up from my food. "Are you tired of me already?"

"Of course not. I was just wondering."

"Assuming I'm in walking condition, I can't leave Spokane until the roads through Montana and Wyoming are clear. That could be as late as April. But I could always stay somewhere else."

"No, I'd like you to stay." She went back to eating. All of a sudden she asked, "Do you believe in an afterlife?"

81

I thought the question a peculiar change of conversation. "Yes."

"Why?" she asked. "There's no evidence of one."

"You don't believe in life after life?"

"I think that death's just death. The grand finale. There's no afterlife, no memory. Nothing."

"That's a depressing thought," I said.

"For some it would be heaven."

"Heaven? To never see our loved ones again?"

"It sounds tragic, but it's not. We'd never know what's gone. A person born blind doesn't miss eyesight."

I just looked at her, wondering why we were having this conversation.

When I didn't respond, she said, "That's what I hope for at least. Sweet oblivion."

After taking another couple of bites, I said, "I met a woman in Davenport who claims to have had a near death experience."

"Those people are crazy."

"She didn't strike me as such."

"So you believe the Bible's version of an after-life with pearly gates and a hell with a lake of fire?"

"Pearly gates and lakes of fire, no. But I believe the spirit and intellect live on, as do relation-ships." I was a little surprised by the strength of my conviction.

She seemed bothered that I didn't echo her belief and her voice turned antagonistic. "What evidence could you or anyone possibly have that something exists past this life?"

I set down my fork. "I'm not arguing with you. Truthfully, for most of my life I wasn't sure what I believed, until . . ." I stopped, not sure of how much I wanted to share.

She was looking at me intensely. "Until what?"

"The day after McKale's funeral I was considering taking my life. Just before I swallowed a handful of pills I heard a voice."

"What kind of voice?"

"I don't know how to explain it. I actually thought someone had spoken to me and I looked around the room. The voice seemed both to have come from inside me and outside me. All I know is that it didn't feel like my own thoughts.

"Then, after the mugging, just before the paramedics revived me, I had another experience. It was something like a dream, except I don't think it was. It was much more lucid. I think I saw McKale."

"Your wife?"

I nodded. "I talked to her. And she told me things."

"What kind of things?"

"She told me that there was a reason we're here on this earth and that there are people I am meant to meet. People whose lives were supposed to intersect with mine." I looked into her eyes. "She told me that I would meet you."

"Me?"

"She told me I would meet 'Angel.' When I woke up in the hospital you were sitting there."

Angel went back to her food, as if she needed time to process what I told her. Finally, she said, "I don't know what to say to that."

"Neither do I."

We finished eating in silence. I got up to do the dishes but she again stopped me. "Please," she said. "Let me do them."

I went to my room and read. When I came out to say goodnight, the kitchen and hall lights were out. She had already gone to bed.

CHAPTER
Ten

Experience has taught me that
the stronger the denial the less
the reason to believe it.

Alan Christoffersen's diary

As I lay in bed, I thought over our conversation. What struck me as peculiar was not so much her opinion, but her anger and disapproval of mine. I have found that the people who shout their opinion the loudest are usually the ones most insecure in their position. I had never seen the dark side of her personality until that night.

Again, Angel was gone when I woke. I ate a breakfast of oatmeal with brown sugar and walnuts, then, focusing on my convalescence, walked out of the house with a new level of confidence knowing that I had already conquered the stairs.

I walked to the sidewalk, then to the end of the property line. I thought that I could have walked further, but being alone, I decided to err on the side of caution and not overdo it. Still, I was pleased. I had made definite progress. If it wasn't for the weather, I figured I could be on my way as early as January.

I shuffled back to the house and climbed the stairs, this time not feeling like I would pass out.

I had just finished getting dressed and was wondering what to do for the day when the doorbell rang. I walked out of my room to answer it.

In the doorway was a woman. She was nicely dressed and had dark red hair that fell to her shoulders. She looked a little older than me, though not by much, and she held a piece of paper in her hand.

"May I help you?" I asked.

She looked surprised. She glanced furtively down at her paper, then back at me. "I'm sorry, does Nicole Mitchell live here?"

"Nicole?" I shook my head. "There's no one here by that name."

She glanced back down the hall at the other doors. "I'm sorry, I must have the wrong apartment. Would you know if she lives in this building?"

I shrugged. "Sorry, I'm new here. I don't know the other tenants."

For a moment she just stood there looking confused about what to do.

"You could knock on the other doors," I suggested.

"Thanks. I'll do that. I'm sorry to bother you."

"No worries." I shut the door.

• • •

Angel arrived home shortly after five. "How was work?" I asked, hoping for better than the day before.

"It was okay," she said softly, then asked, "How was yours?"

"Good," I said.

She nodded. "I picked up a rotisserie chicken on the way home. Do you like stuffing? I have Stove Top."

"I love stuffing," I said, happy that she was in a better mood than she was the last time I'd seen her.

While she cooked the stuffing, I set the table and filled our glasses with water. A few minutes later we sat down to eat.

"I'm sorry I was so moody last night," she said. "I sometimes get that way when my sugars are off."

"No problem," I said.

"I just didn't want you to think I was trying to push you out. I'm really glad you're here."

"I didn't take it that way," I said. "And I'm glad I'm here too."

She looked relieved. "So, what did you do today?"

"I got caught up in my journal," I said. "And I watched Judge Judy. That woman is hardcore."

Angel grinned. "That's probably why she's so popular. Did you walk?"

"I made it to the edge of the yard and back."

"Congratulations. You're making real progress."

"I've come a long way since that first walk to the bathroom." I pulled some chicken from the breast with my fork. "I've been meaning to ask you, when does Spokane get its first snow?"

"I haven't been through a winter here since I was a kid, but I think that they usually have snow by the middle of November."

"My goal is to make it around the block before the snow flies."

Angel was cutting meat from the chicken's breast and said without looking up, "You'll make it. You're doing great."

I took another bite. "Do you have a neighbor named Nicole?"

Angel abruptly looked up. "Why?"

"A woman came by this afternoon looking for someone named Nicole."

"What woman?"

"Just some woman."

"What did she look like?"

"She was probably just a little older than us. She was nicely dressed and had long red hair."

"What did you tell her?"

"I told her that Nicole didn't live here."

Angel looked at me for a moment, then went back to her meal nearly as abruptly as she had stopped eating. "No, there's no one here with that name. Would you like some more stuffing?"

I looked at her quizzically, then handed her my plate. "Sure."

After dinner I convinced Angel to let me help her with the dishes after which she made popcorn and we went out to watch our movie. *City Lights* hadn't arrived yet, so we jumped up to number seventy-five, *Dances with Wolves*, directed by and starring Kevin Costner.

I had seen the movie before—twice, I think—but it had been more than a decade.

McKale and I had watched it together. I remember that she cried at the end, which wasn't all that surprising since she cried at Hallmark card commercials.

Later that year the movie won seven Academy Awards, including Best Picture. Much of the film was shot in South Dakota and Wyoming, two of the states I would pass through when I was walking again.

Dances with Wolves is one of the longer movies on the top hundred list, nearly four hours in length, and Angel fell asleep long before it ended. As the credits rolled up the screen, I leaned forward and gently shook her. "Hey, it's over."

Her eyelids fluttered, then she looked up at me as if unsure of who I was. Then she blinked a few times and her eyes widened. "Oh. Is the movie over?"

"Yes."

She rubbed her eyes. "How did it end?"

"The Indians lost."

"Thought so," she said, standing.

I took a deep breath, then without help lifted myself up from the couch. I still had to take a moment to catch my breath.

"I could have helped you," Angel said sleepily, barely stable on her own legs.

"I know." I started walking toward my room. "Good night," I said.

"Good night, Kevin."

I looked at her. "Kevin?"

"Alan," she said quickly.

I grinned. "Sorry, I'm not Costner."

"Costner?" she asked, then nodded. "Oh right. Good night."

I woke in the middle of the night. My room was dark, and I rolled over to look at the radio-alarm clock on the nightstand next to my bed. 3:07. I groaned, then lay back, wondering why I had woken so early. Then I heard it, a soft, muffled groan. My first thought was that it was a tomcat outside my window, until I realized it was coming from inside the apartment.

For several minutes, I lay still and listened. The noise sounded like crying. I pushed myself up and climbed out of bed, quietly opening my door. The sound was coming from Angel's room. I walked over to her door and put my ear against it.

Angel was sobbing, though the noise was muffled, as if she were holding a pillow against her face. The sound of her in pain was heart-wrenching. I stood there for a moment, wanting to comfort her but unsure of what to do. Maybe she didn't want my help.

After several minutes her sobbing decreased to a whimper, then faded altogether. I hobbled back to my bed, my mind filled with questions. The longer I was with her, the more I realized how little I knew her. The truth is, I didn't know her at all.

CHAPTER
Eleven

We're all moons. Sometimes our
dark sides overshadow our light.

Alan Christoffersen's diary

The next week passed quietly as I settled into
my new routine. I noticed something peculiar
about my emotional state. Somehow the change
of setting helped me keep my mind off
McKale, as if I could deceive myself that I was
only away on a business trip, and she was home
waiting for me. Or, maybe it was because there
was nothing familiar in my surroundings to
remind me of her. Either way, I welcomed the
emotional respite.

I walked a little further every day. And every
day after my walk I studied my road atlas at
length, marking it with a yellow highlighter pen,
comparing roads and routes to best determine
my next course.

I decided that when my body and the weather
permitted, I would walk east along Interstate 90
through Coeur d'Alene, Idaho, then head south
into Yellowstone National Park, exiting the east
gate on my way to Rapid City, South Dakota. My
route was probably neither the shortest nor the

easiest. I had been to Yellowstone as a child and I just wanted to see the park again.

I didn't plan my route past South Dakota for the same reason I hadn't planned the first leg of my trip past Spokane: something my father had taught me. Whenever I got frustrated with a difficult task, my father would say, "How do you eat an elephant?" I'd look at him as if he'd lost his mind, then he'd say, "One bite at a time." Rapid City, a little over 700 miles from Spokane, was my next bite.

I talked Angel into letting me take over the cooking. Compared to Angel, I wasn't much of a chef, but I could handle myself in a kitchen. In my previous life I was a better cook than McKale, who claimed that the only thing she could make in the kitchen were reservations.

Our carousel of movies continued fairly regularly and our entertainment couldn't have been more eclectic. The list took us from Westerns to classics to science fiction. In one week we watched *The Gold Rush*, *Wuthering Heights*, *Ben-Hur*, *Forrest Gump*, and *The French Connection*.

I started having reservations about the American Film Institute's rankings. *Forrest Gump* was a stretch for me, but—with all due respect to Dustin Hoffman—*Tootsie*?

I never said anything to Angel about the night I had heard her crying. I figured that if and when she wanted to talk about what was hurting her, she would. But it made me wonder about her and her past, which I knew nothing about, and she remained stingy in sharing.

Outside of her occasional bouts of moodiness, she was nothing but kind to me and spoke encouragingly about my progress. But underneath her veneer of hospitality there was a chasm of deep sadness and loneliness—emotions I understood all too well.

What worried me is that I sensed the gap was growing, as if each day she took one step back from me and the rest of the world. I had no idea how to cross the gap or even if I should try, but I couldn't help but worry about her.

Ten days after being released from the hospital, Angel drove me back to Sacred Heart's outpatient clinic so they could remove my stitches. While we were there, we dropped by the ICU to see Norma. Sadly, it was her day off.

My muscle tone was slowly returning as my wounds healed, and by the end of my second week at Angel's I could get off the couch or climb the stairs without considering either journalworthy. I wasn't about to compete in the Ironman, but for the time being, it was enough.

On November 11, I reached my first major goal. I walked to the corner of our block, then turned south and walked to the end of the street. Even though Angel and I had driven past this corner on the way to her house, there was something different about encountering the place on my own legs.

A Montessori school took up the back half of the block, and there were a few dozen young boys on the school's backfield playing football.

I stopped to watch them, lacing my fingers through the cold chain-link fence. The boys wore long navy blue jerseys with big white helmets that made them look like bobble-head dolls.

I felt remarkably liberated to be outside and this far from home, and I took my time walking back. Walking around the block was a far cry from the twenty to thirty miles I'd been putting in prior to the attack, but it didn't matter. Snows had already hit Wyoming and Montana, and the east entrance of Yellowstone was already closed to traffic. I wasn't going anywhere soon.

CHAPTER
Twelve

Angel's landlord came to the door and asked for Nicole. What am I missing?

Alan Christoffersen's diary

The first measurable snow in Spokane fell on the fourteenth. The snowfall was deeper than I had anticipated—nearly five inches—and the sidewalks were completely buried. The good news was that the weatherman said it would be gone by the end of the week.

Instead of walking outside, I did some light calisthenics, then found an aerobics channel on television, which I followed along with at the lowest impact level.

As I was exercising, I could hear someone going up and down the walks with a snow blower. I parted the curtains and looked out. An elderly man was clearing the walks. He wore a brown parka, a knit scarf, and a hunting cap with earflaps, which he had pulled down and tied under his chin.

I thought he was a little old to be clearing the walks and, had I been able, I would have gone out and helped him.

About a half hour later, as I was finishing my

second workout, there was a knock on the apartment door. I opened it to find the elderly gentleman standing in the doorway, his hat and shoulders flocked with snow. "Hello, is Nicole in?"

I looked at him quizzically. "No, Angel Arnell lives here."

His brow furrowed, then he said, "Oh, then is Angel here?"

"No, she's at work."

"I'm Bill Dodd, I own this place. I just need to do a quick look-through of the apartment."

I was a little apprehensive about letting a complete stranger into Angel's apartment, especially after he had called Angel by the wrong name, but he looked harmless enough, and he had just plowed the walks. Besides, he smelled of Old Spice cologne. How bad could you be wearing Old Spice?

"Come in," I said, stepping back from the door. "I'm sure she won't mind."

He stomped his feet off at the door then walked inside. He took less than ten minutes to look around the place. As he was leaving he asked, "What's your name?"

"Alan."

He took off one of his mittens and put out his hand. "Pleasure to know you, Alan."

I shook his hand. "Nice to meet you too."

"Would you mind telling Angel I came by?

97

And tell her thanks for the get-well card. It made me laugh."

"Glad to."

He stopped outside the doorway. "She's a great gal, Angel. I hate to see her go. I have some people interested in taking the place, but if she changes her mind, I'm more than happy to keep her. Wish I had more renters like her."

I was surprised by this news. "When does her lease expire?"

"February first. She's got a couple more months." He put his mitten back on. "Goodbye."

"Bye." I shut the door. "That's weird," I said aloud. Angel hadn't said a word to me about moving.

That night as we were eating dinner, I told Angel about the visit.

"Your landlord came by today. He cleared the walks."

"Bill?"

"I think that was his name."

"I love Bill. I don't know why he insists on clearing the walks himself. He has plenty of money and he's eighty-two years old." She said grimly, "I think he's trying to have a heart attack."

I looked up from my spaghetti. "You sound serious."

"I'm only half kidding. He lost his wife two years ago. I don't think he wants to live anymore."

"I can understand that," I said.

She either missed my comment or ignored it. "He collects model electric trains. I've been to his house. His entire basement is one huge train track. It's actually quite impressive. You'll have to see it sometime." She leaned forward. "So what did he have to say?"

"He said 'Thank you for the get-well card.' And he also said that if you change your mind about moving he's happy to keep the apartment for you."

"Oh."

I was hoping she would say more about the moving part, but she didn't. I took another bite of spaghetti then asked, "Are you moving?"

She hesitated. "When I first moved here, I wasn't sure how long I'd be staying, so I only signed a six-month lease. I'll give him a call on my lunch break tomorrow." She went back to eating.

"It's kind of a weird coincidence," I said, "but when I opened the door, he didn't ask for you. He asked for Nicole."

Angel didn't look up.

"I just thought that was kind of strange," I said, "after that woman came by the other day looking for—"

She cut me off. "I don't know any Nicole." She took another bite of spaghetti.

I looked at her for a moment then went back to my meal.

When the silence became uncomfortable, she asked, "Did you walk today?"

"No. I did aerobics off the television."

"Sweatin' to the oldies?"

"Something like that," I said.

"So, what movie are we on tonight?" she asked. I had become the expert on the list.

"Sixty-nine. *Shane*."

"Is that the one about the Harlem detective?"

I looked at her a moment, then smiled wryly. "That's *Shaft*. *Shane* is a Western with Jack Palance."

"Close," she said.

We both burst out laughing. Nothing more was said that night about Bill or Nicole.

CHAPTER
Thirteen

People aren't wired to be alone.
Even in the stressful population of
prison, solitary confinement is still
considered a cruel punishment.

Alan Christoffersen's diary

I was eating breakfast the next morning when it suddenly struck me what was wrong with Angel's apartment. There were no photographs. Not one. No snapshots of a mother, father, friend or sibling. There was no image of another human in the entire apartment.

In fact, there was no evidence that this woman had any connection with humanity at all. That was true of her speech as well. In all our conversations she had never once mentioned family or friends, not even in anger.

No, there had been *one* picture. I don't know how I remembered this, but when I had stopped to help her outside Davenport, I remembered seeing a picture of a young boy hanging from her rearview mirror next to a crucifix.

What kind of person lives her life like Eleanor Rigby, then invites a complete stranger to live in her home for an indefinite period of time? Or, was that precisely why she had invited me—so she would have someone to be with? Maybe. People *need* people. So where were they in Angel's world?

My questions about Angel were stacking up. Her crying at night, our conversation about death and her hope for oblivion, the coincidence of two people asking for Nicole—and Angel's peculiar reaction when I told her. *Who was Angel and why was I here?*

My intuition told me that whatever was bothering Angel had something to do with this Nicole woman, but I had no idea who she was. I didn't even know her last name. Unfortunately, I hadn't been paying attention when the woman who had come asking about Nicole had mentioned it. Why would I? At the time, the encounter meant no more to me than a wrong number.

It occurred to me that perhaps others in the building might know something about her, so I decided to talk to them. I had my first chance that afternoon.

I had increased my walking to twice a day. A little after 2 P.M. I was stretching in the foyer when I ran into one of Angel's neighbors, the young woman I had passed coming out of the apartment on my first walk. She came slowly into the building with her head down. She jumped a little when she saw me. "You startled me."

"Sorry," I said.

"No, it's just I hardly ever see anyone here."

"I know what you mean. It's really quiet. Are all the apartments rented?"

"You wouldn't know it, but they are. Bill doesn't rent to anyone noisier than he is. So we're all church mice."

"Bill the landlord?"

"Yes."

I reached out my hand. "I'm Alan Christoffersen."

She shook my hand. "I'm Christine Wilcox. It's nice to meet you. You're in apartment three?"

I nodded. "I just moved in with Angel a couple of weeks ago. Have you lived here long?"

"Long for me. I've been here a couple years. I'm a senior at Gonzaga."

"I guessed you were a student by the backpack," I said.

"Standard uniform," she said.

"Two years," I repeated. "So you probably know all the tenants here?"

"Yes. But not well. Everyone pretty much keeps to themselves."

"Maybe you could help me. Was there ever a tenant here named Nicole?"

Her brow furrowed. "Nicole? Not since I've been here. Why?"

"A woman came by the other day looking for Nicole."

"Oh yeah, she left a note at my door. No. Not since I've been here. But you could ask Bill."

"Thanks. Maybe I'll do that. It's nice meeting you, Christine."

"My pleasure. Have a good run." She reached into her pocket for her keys. "Oh, and say 'hi' to Angel for me. We keep threatening to get together, but every time I've come over, she doesn't answer. I'm starting to think she's avoiding me." Christine unlocked her door and opened it. "Have a good day."

"You too."

She disappeared inside her apartment. I walked out the front door to start my walk.

That night I made clam chowder for supper. While we were eating, Angel said, "May I ask you about your wife?"

"Sure."

"What was she like?"

I smiled sadly. "She was perfect. I mean, for me she was. I should say that she was perfectly flawed. We both lost our mothers at a young age, and neither of us had siblings, so we held to each other. Our broken edges fit. I can't imagine loving anyone as much as I loved her."

"That's how it should be. I think it's rare. Why are you walking to Key West?"

"You want to know why I'm walking to Key West, or why I'm walking?"

"Both."

"I chose Key West because it was far. I'm walking because after I lost McKale, I also lost my home, my cars, and my business. Walking away just seemed the prudent thing to do."

"Sometimes we need to run away," Angel said, nodding as if she understood. "How did you lose your business?"

"I was betrayed by my partner. While I was taking care of McKale, he stole all my clients and started his own firm."

"That's reprehensible."

"I thought so."

"What's his name?"

"Kyle Craig," I said slowly. "Never trust anyone with two first names."

"Do you hate him?"

The question made me think. "I suppose so, if I think about it. But truthfully, I don't think much of him and I don't think that much about him. Dwelling on him would make him a bigger part of my life than I want him to be."

"That's wise," she said. She took another bite of soup, then asked, "Do you hate the kid who stabbed you?"

"He's dead. There's no one to hate."

"A lot of people hate dead people."

"That's true," I said. I leaned back and gazed into her eyes. "Is there anyone you hate?"

"I could name a few people."

"Anyone in particular?"

She didn't answer immediately, and when she did, there was a strange tone to her voice. "Probably me."

CHAPTER
Fourteen

As difficult as walking is to me
these days, I still seem to have no
trouble walking into trouble.

Alan Christoffersen's diary

Spokane's second major snowfall came early in the morning on November 17. That afternoon I walked twice around the block with almost no pain, except when I almost slipped and caught myself.

As I came back down the road to the apartment, I saw Bill, the landlord, pushing his snow blower up our sidewalk. I stopped on the walk near him, giving him a short wave. "Hi, Bill."

He cupped his ear.

"Hi!" I shouted. When he got up to me, he bent over and switched off the snow blower. He was huffing from exertion and his glasses were frosted with snow. He wiped them with the back of his mitten. "What can I do for you?"

"I'm Alan Christoffersen. We met a few days ago."

He gazed intently at me, as if trying to remember.

"I'm Angel's friend. Did Angel ever get back to you on the lease?"

I could tell that he still wasn't sure who I was. "No. Not yet."

"She says that she plans to."

"Well, tell her not to wait too long. I've got a bird in the hand."

"I'll do that." He started to bend over to restart his blower when I asked, "May I ask you something?"

"You just did."

I ignored the comment. "A few days ago when you came by the apartment you asked for Nicole. Who is Nicole?"

A grim look crossed his face. "I think that if Angel wanted you to know, she'd tell you herself."

"I'm trying to help Angel. I may be her closest friend."

He frowned. "If you were a close friend, you'd already know." He reached down and pulled on the rope to start the blower. The machine roared to life on the first pull. I stepped out of the way as the old man stormed by in a cascade of snow.

That evening Angel arrived home from work a little later than usual, and it was already completely dark out. It was obvious that she'd had another bad day, as she barely spoke to me. *Moody again,* I thought. Sitting down to dinner, I asked, "Are you okay?"

She nodded but didn't speak.

"We're on movie number sixty-eight, *An American in Paris*."

She didn't respond. The only sounds from our meal were the clinking of fork and knife. Once again the silence became painful.

The fact that she was avoiding eye contact with me made me wonder if the problem had something to do with me.

Finally, I broke the silence. "Thanksgiving is only a week away. Do you have any plans?"

"No."

"Do you want to go out?"

"I don't celebrate Thanksgiving," she said. Back to silence. Halfway through the meal I gave up. "Okay, did I do something to offend you?"

She slowly looked up, as if deciding whether or not to answer. Finally, she said, "I talked to my landlord this afternoon. He said that you talked to him."

"He was out clearing the walk."

"I would appreciate it if you would stay out of my personal affairs." She stood up and walked to her bedroom. I sat there in a stupor. After a few more minutes I put our plates in the sink and went to my room. We both went to bed without another word.

That night I woke again to her crying.

CHAPTER
Fifteen

I can see clearly now.
How could I have been so obtuse?

Alan Christoffersen's diary

The next morning, for the first time since I'd arrived, I considered leaving. I wouldn't be able to continue my walk, I wasn't ready and neither was the weather, but I could always find some-place else in Spokane to stay.

I looked through the phone book and found an extended-stay hotel just 2 miles from the house. Angel didn't have a phone other than her cell phone, so I couldn't call to check on vacancies, but at just 2 miles I thought I could make the walk.

As I began to mentally plan my departure, I stopped myself. *After all Angel had done for me, could I really just walk out on her?* I knew I couldn't. I was worried about her.

I also still believed in the vision, that I was meant to meet Angel. Selfishly, I had assumed that meeting her was for my benefit, just like the other "angels" I had met so far on my walk, but now I realized that maybe I was sent here for her.

It seemed to me that Angel was on a slope of sorts, and I didn't know where or how far it fell. What I did know was that I, being the only one in her life, was probably her only hope. I decided to stay as long as there was a chance of helping.

There hadn't been any new snow for two days and the streets and walks were reasonably clear, so I decided to try my first long-distance excursion and walk with my empty pack 2½ miles to the outskirts of the suburb, then back, a journey of 5 miles in all.

My walk started out well, at least for the first couple miles, but after that my thighs and calves were burning, not so much from the injury as from being out of shape. Even empty, the pack seemed heavier than I remembered. I was moving at a turtle's pace when I arrived back on Nora Street, grateful to be home. On my way inside the house I stopped and picked up the mail. There was a postcard from the cable company marked RETURN TO SENDER.

A Friendly reminder from Larcom Cable

Dear Valued Customer,
    Your Larcom Cable account will expire in just 90 days.
    We value your business, so if you re-subscribe now we'll bonus you two

months of Spokane's greatest entertainment value absolutely FREE. Plus, we'll
send you a coupon for a FREE large,
2-topping pizza from PIZZA HUT.

This is a limited time offer, so act
now to keep the excitement coming!

Across the bottom of the card were scrawled the
words *Please cancel my account, I won't be
needing it.*

I checked the postage mark. The card had been
sent just three days earlier.

Angel came home late from work again, and I
expected another night of uncomfortable silence.
Instead, as soon as she walked in, she called my
name. "Alan."

I walked from the kitchen to the hallway. She
smiled sweetly when she saw me. "Hi."

Her complete change in temperament surprised
me. "Hi."

"Do you want to go out tonight?"

"I made dinner."

"Can we freeze it? I'd like to take you out."

"All right," I said, a little bemused.

"How does Chinese sound? The Asian Star has
fabulous potstickers and their walnut shrimp is
life-changing."

"Say no more," I said.

We put dinner in the refrigerator, then drove

immediately to the restaurant, which was near the university and crowded with students. After the waitress had taken our orders, Angel said, "I miss going to school. I love the energy."

"How long did you go?"

"I had to drop out my junior year, when I . . ." She stopped mid-sentence. She looked down for a moment, then back up into my eyes. She looked soft, full of contrition. "I'm sorry I've been so irritable lately. You must feel like you're living with a crazy woman."

"No," I said. "But I've been worried about you. If I can do anything for you—if you need to talk, I'm a good listener."

"Thank you," she said, but nothing more.

I cleared my throat. "So, I've been thinking. I would really like to prepare Thanksgiving dinner."

"I don't really celebrate Thanksgiving," she said.

"I know. But maybe you could make an exception, so I could thank you for all that you've done for me."

"You don't need to do that. Besides, I have to work Thursday."

"We'll eat when you get back."

She didn't respond; rather, she looked quiet, as if suddenly lost in thought. Then she glanced up at me. "Okay," she said, relenting. "That sounds fun."

"Thanksgiving it is."

After dinner we stopped by the video store for the next video on our list. They didn't have the movie we were supposed to be watching, *The Third Man*, starring Joseph Cotten and Orson Welles, but they did have number fifty-six: *M*A*S*H*.

As a child I rarely missed the TV series spawned by the movie, but I had never seen the original with Donald Sutherland and Elliott Gould.

Not surprisingly, the movie was darker and edgier than the television series, with an anti-religious agenda about as subtle as a mankini.

About halfway through the movie there is a scene where Waldowski, the camp dentist, decides to commit suicide.

Predictably, Hawkeye and Trapper John make a joke of it and offer Waldowski the "black pill," which is actually harmless but which Waldowski believes will bring sudden death. At the scene's climax (a spoof on da Vinci's *Last Supper*) the group gathers for Waldowski's death, and a soldier sings the movie's title song: "*Suicide Is Painless*."

My own recent contemplations about life and death rendered the segment uncomfortable. I glanced over at Angel to see if she thought it was funny. To my surprise, she was crying.

Suddenly, I understood what was going on. How had I missed the obvious?

CHAPTER
Sixteen

If the road to hell is paved with
good intentions, I laid a pretty
good stretch of asphalt today.
I suppose I've done enough damage.
It's time for me to leave.

Alan Christoffersen's diary

The classic signs of suicide were all there, as glaring as a Las Vegas casino sign. The expiration of her lease and cable, her quiet, abiding sadness, her outspoken hope for oblivion. The surrendering of her possessions, like the sapphire necklace she'd attempted to give to Norma at the hospital. Her intentions were obvious—what I didn't know was *why*.

As the production credits rolled up the screen at the end of the movie, Angel switched on the lamp and stood. "Ready for bed?"

"I'd like to talk," I said.

The gravity of my tone was not lost on her. She looked at me nervously. "It's kind of late."

"It's important."

She looked at me for a moment, then sat down on the sofa. "Okay," she said, knitting her fingers together. "What do you want to talk about?"

115

I moved closer to her and put my hand on hers. "I'm not sure how to approach this, so I'll just say what's on my mind. First, I want you to know that I care about you deeply. I am very grateful for all you've done to help me."

"I care about you too," she said, her brows knit with anxiety.

"Clearly. You've been very good to me. I also know that something is very wrong."

"I know it seems that way, but everything's fine," she said. "Really. I've just been a little emotional lately."

"Angel, it's more than that." I looked into her eyes, then slowly breathed out. "I need you to be completely honest with me. Who is Nicole?"

She looked at me incredulously. "I told you to stay out of my affairs," she said sharply.

"I can't help you if you're not honest with me. Does this Nicole have something to do with why you're so sad?"

"You have no idea what you're asking."

"You're right, I don't. But I want to know. I want to help. I think that's why we were led to each other."

Her expression turned fierce. "We weren't *led* to each other. There is no fate. There is no God. There is only chaos and chance. You're here because of coincidence."

"I'm here because I stopped to help you and you knew you could trust me."

She began to cry.

"I know why you came back to Spokane," I said.

"Enlighten me," she replied angrily. "Why did I come back?"

"You came home to die."

She just stared at me for a moment then stood. "Stop it."

"Angel—"

"Leave me alone."

"No," I said.

"I made a mistake coming for you," she shouted.

"You found exactly what you were looking for."

"And what was that?"

"Hope," I said.

She was quiet for a moment, then said, "What I do with my life is my business and mine alone." She stormed off, stopping in the threshold of her room. "And don't talk to me about hope. There is no hope. The only hope is oblivion." She slammed the door behind her.

From the couch I could hear her crying. I walked over to her door, then pressed my forehead against it.

"I really do care, Angel."

"No one cares. Go away."

"You're wrong."

"Go away, please."

I went to my room and lay on top of the covers. It was more than an hour before I fell asleep.

Angel didn't speak to me for the next three days. She came home late each night and went straight to her room. I tried to get her to talk to me, but all my attempts were met with hostility. I feared every day for her. Most of all, I feared she might hurt herself. I had failed in my quest to help her. I had more than failed—I felt like I had pushed her closer to the brink.

By Tuesday afternoon I couldn't stand the silence and tension anymore, and I was now sure that it wasn't going to get better. Around three in the afternoon I made up my mind. For better or for worse, I was leaving.

But not without saying goodbye. I owed her that. I packed up my things and waited for Angel to come home.

CHAPTER
Seventeen

My father used to say that people
are like books: unknown until
they're opened. Until Angel,
I have never felt so illiterate.

Alan Christoffersen's diary

I was sitting on the couch when Angel's Malibu
pulled up to the curb. My pack was full and
leaning against the sofa. I stood as she entered
the apartment. She froze when she saw me,
then looked back and forth between my pack
and me. "What's going on?" she asked.

I lifted my pack. "I'm leaving," I said. "I was
just waiting for you to come home so I could
say goodbye."

"Why?"

I walked up to her. "Thank you for everything
you've done for me. I'm sorry that things turned
out the way they did. I would do anything to
change it, except pretend things are okay."

She just looked at me, speechless.

"I hope you know that I didn't mean to hurt
you. I would never hurt you. You're a beautiful
soul."

She swallowed. "Where are you going to go?"

"You don't need to worry about that. You've done enough. I left some money on the table." I leaned forward and kissed her on the cheek. "Good luck, Angel. I hope you find peace. I don't know anyone who deserves it more."

As I walked to the door, her eyes welled up with tears. "Who will take care of you?"

"I can take care of myself."

I stepped out into the hallway and she followed me out. "Then who will take care of me?"

I looked at her. "No one, if you won't let them. I'm not going to stay and watch you destroy yourself. I can't. I care too much about you to do that." I looked down and adjusted my pack, securing the waistband. When I looked back up, she was covering her eyes and crying.

"Good luck," I said.

I walked out the front door of the building and down the stairs. There was a light snow falling, reflecting the dying sun in the cool twilight. Halfway down the walk I heard the door open behind me.

"Alan."

I didn't turn back.

Then in a trembling voice she shouted, "I'm Nicole."

I stopped and turned around. Tears were streaming down her face. "I'm Nicole," she said. She fell to her knees. "Please don't leave me. You're my only hope." She dropped her head, her hands clenching her hair. "Please, help me."

I shrugged off my pack, then walked back as fast as I could to her. I knelt down and put my arms around her, pulling her into me. She put her face against my chest and wept.

CHAPTER
Eighteen

If you plan to burst someone's bubble, be sure to have both hands cupped beneath them.

Alan Christoffersen's diary

We were both covered in snow when I brought her inside and sat her on the couch. She cried for nearly fifteen minutes, then she went completely silent, occasionally whimpering or shuddering.

When she could speak, she said in a strained voice, "You asked what I was going to do when I finished the movies. I was going to watch the last movie, then I was going to go out and eat whatever I wanted. A big banana split with caramel and whipped cream and a cherry." She looked up into my eyes. "Then I was going to come home and overdose on insulin."

She said it so calmly that it took a moment for her plan to sink in.

She continued, "It's easy to kill yourself when you're diabetic. No one would even know it was suicide. I'd just slip off into a hyperglycemic coma and be dead before anyone found me."

I rubbed my thumb over her cheek. "Why would you take your life?"

"You don't know my life."

"I know you."

"No. I've lied to you about everything. Even my name. Killing my name was the beginning of killing myself. Nicole was already dead to me."

"What happened, Nicole?"

She put her head down. "You don't want to know."

I put my hand under her chin and gently lifted it until she was looking into my eyes.

She exhaled deeply. "My life fell apart when I was eighteen. I had just started college, with a film studies major." She shook her head. ". . . There's a useful career for you."

I squeezed her hand.

"I was still living at home when my mother took a new job and got in with a different group of people. They changed her. She started hanging out with them after work, going to bars and clubs. She started coming home drunk. My dad just put up with it, thinking it was a phase. But it wasn't. After a couple months she told my father that she wanted a divorce. Dad was devastated. He begged her to stay, but she'd already made up her mind. After twenty-two years of marriage, she treated him like a stranger. My father had always struggled with depression, so when she threw him out, he couldn't handle it." Her eyes welled up. "One night he took his life."

Nicole wiped her eyes. "That time is just a blur to me. Everything was in commotion. I stopped going to school, my sister ran off with her boyfriend, then my mother informed me that she was moving in with one of her friends so I'd have to find someplace else to live. I dropped out of school and got a job.

"I wasn't really qualified for anything, so I took the day shift at a Dairy Queen. That's where I met Kevin. He was the owner. He was a lot older than me, almost fifteen years older."

She looked at me with a pained expression. "It seemed like such a good thing. He owned his own business. He had a house and a nice car. Most of all, he paid attention to me. I mean, I had to pay for it, he did whatever he wanted with me, but I didn't care. I didn't care about anything. I just wanted someone to want me.

"One night he told me that he was engaged to someone else, but he didn't love her. He loved me."

Nicole wiped her eyes. "I knew it was wrong, I should have left him, but I didn't. I was so afraid of being alone again. He asked me to marry him. I didn't think about that other woman or how much it would hurt her. I didn't even worry about his unfaithfulness. I just wanted him for my own, so I told him yes.

"Kevin and his fiancée had already started making wedding plans when he called the engagement off. His mother, Barbara, was livid. She wouldn't even acknowledge me.

"A couple weeks before we got married, I was alone with Barbara when she cornered me and asked me what I was trying to do. I didn't understand her question. I said, 'I'm marrying your son.' She said, 'You cheated with an engaged man. You're nothing but a tramp.' I started to cry. I told her that I didn't know he was engaged. She called me a liar. Then she said, 'Are you stupid enough to think he really wants *you?* You're just a little plaything for him. As soon as he tires of you, he'll throw you out like yesterday's garbage.'

"Then she pulled out her checkbook and offered me five thousand dollars to leave and never come back. I couldn't believe it. When I turned her down, she said, 'Don't think this is going to last. You'll never be part of this family.'

"From then on she did everything she could to make my life miserable. We got married, but it was one of the worst days of my life. Barbara didn't say a word to me all day.

"I thought she'd eventually accept me, but things only got worse. Every time Kevin spent time with her, he'd come home and give me the silent treatment. She'd poison him. I started begging him to stay away from her, but he just got mad and said I didn't understand her and that I should be grateful for all she did for us.

"She owned him, emotionally and financially. She owned the controlling rights to the Dairy Queen. Before we got married, I had to sign a prenuptial agreement relinquishing all claims to his money, or else, Kevin said, she'd force him out of the business and we'd be broke. I think I signed the agreement to prove to Barbara that I wasn't a gold digger. I didn't care about the agreement, I wasn't after his money. I wanted to be loved. But it didn't make any difference. She got it in her mind that I was trash and nothing was going to change that.

"Then I got pregnant with Aiden. I thought having a grandchild would finally convince Barbara that I wasn't going anywhere, but she worked even harder to break us up. She would bring women home to meet Kevin. Can you believe that? She'd actually bring women home to meet her married son. And there I was, pregnant and feeling unattractive. He'd say, 'I'm married, Mom,' and she'd roll her eyes and say, 'For now.' "

"How did you know she did that?" I asked.

"Kevin told me about it. At first Kevin stood up for me—at least as much as he dared—but after Aiden was born, things changed. The truth is, Kevin didn't want the responsibility of fatherhood and he blamed me for that. He stopped coming home. He'd go out playing cards and drinking with his friends almost every night. "I assumed they were all male friends until someone told me that they'd seen him with another woman.

"After that we got into a fight, and he said that I'd gotten pregnant just to trap him. I said, 'Trap you into what? We're already married!' He said, 'For now.'

"He apologized the next day, but you can't really take that back. I had no one but my son. So I built my entire life around him."

Her demeanor changed and there was a far-away look in her eyes. "On his fourth birthday I picked him up early from preschool to take him to the zoo. We stopped at the Dairy Queen to get an ice-cream cone. Kevin was there and we got in another big fight. I was so angry that I grabbed Aiden and left." She paused and her eyes welled up with tears. "I pulled out of the parking lot without looking. This car came out of nowhere. The police said the driver was going nearly eighty miles per hour in a forty-mile-per-hour zone.

"He hit my car on the driver's side, about a foot behind me, where Aiden was in his car seat. It killed Aiden instantly." She began to sob.

"I had to be pulled from the car by the Jaws of Life. I was cut all over. I had internal bleeding and more than twenty broken bones." She looked down. "Unfortunately, they saved my life."

She was quiet for a while, unable to speak. When she could, I had to strain to hear. "While I was in the hospital, only two people came to see me. One was the mother of the man who was driving the car. He was killed in the crash. This woman blamed me. I lay there, unable to move, while she screamed at me. Finally, a nurse heard her and called security. They had to drag her out.

"The other person was Barbara. She came to tell me that I had killed her grandchild and it was God's punishment for stealing someone else's husband. She said she wished that I had died instead."

My eyes welled up. "What did you say to her?"

She looked up at me. "I said that I wished I had too.

"I was still in the hospital when I got served divorce papers. My wrists were broken, the nurse had to open the envelope and read them to me."

She squinted, forcing a stream of tears down her cheeks. "I decided my life wasn't worth anything, so I came back to Spokane to end it.

"When I met you, I had just been to Seattle. I wanted to see the ocean again. I wanted to stand on Bullman Beach and feel the wind in my hair and listen to the waves. Do you know Bullman Beach?"

I shook my head.

"It's near Neah Bay, on the west side of Olympic National Park."

"I know where that is," I said. "I drove through there once. It's beautiful."

"When I was seven, my family stayed there at a little inn on the beach. I was happy then. I wanted to see it one last time." She exhaled deeply. "My mother had a nickname for me back then."

"What was it?"

She looked up into my eyes. "Angel."

CHAPTER
Nineteen

We humans are born egocentric.
The sky thunders and children believe
that God is mad at them for something
they've done—parents divorce and
children believe it's their fault for not
being good enough. Growing up
means putting aside our egocentricity
for truth.
Still, some people cling to this childish
mind-set. As painful as their self-
flagellation may be, they'd rather
believe their crises are their fault so
they can believe they have control.
In doing so they make fools and
false Gods of themselves.

Alan Christoffersen's diary

I held Nicole for more than an hour. She cuddled into me like a little girl seeking shelter, which might be close to the truth. At one point she began crying again, which she did for nearly twenty minutes before she fell silent. When she finally sat back up, she was soft and vulnerable.

"Do you think God was punishing me?" she asked.

I shook my head. "Aiden's death wasn't your fault. It belongs to the man driving that speeding car. But I understand your question, because, for a while, I wondered the same thing about McKale.

"I had an employee who one day came into work crying. Her doctor had just informed her that she couldn't have children. She said to me, 'It's because God's punishing me.' I asked her why God was punishing her. She said, 'Because I haven't been going to church.' That very morning I had read an article in the newspaper about a drug addict, prostitute, who was arrested for putting her newborn baby in a Dumpster. I said to my friend, 'You're telling me that God won't give you a baby because you missed church, but he gave a baby to that prostitute to kill?' It doesn't make any sense."

"Then you don't believe God punishes us?"

"I don't know if He does or not. But I don't believe in a God I can control," I said. "It seems to me that He is much more interested in helping us than in condemning us. I believe that's why when we're in need, he puts people in our path. Think about it, doesn't it seem peculiar that someone who understands what it means to lose everything ends up in your home exactly when you needed him most?"

After a moment she said, "Yes."

"Just six weeks ago I was on my knees holding two bottles of painkillers and a bottle of whiskey, ready to end it all. And now here I am with you. It's miraculous."

She looked down for a long time. "How do you live when you don't want to live anymore?"

How many times had I asked myself the same thing? I thought. "One day at a time," I said softly. "One day at a time."

That evening we didn't eat. We never even left the couch. I held Nicole until she fell asleep in my arms. I wasn't strong enough yet to carry her, so I woke her and helped her into her room. I pulled back the covers, pulled off her shoes, then tucked her in bed with her clothes still on. I kissed her on the forehead, then went to my own room. I lay in bed replaying our conversation over in my mind. I wondered what Nicole would do in the morning.

CHAPTER
Twenty

The first step of a journey
is always the longest.

Alan Christoffersen's diary

I woke a little after sunrise. I was contemplating the night before when there was a knock on my door. "Come in," I said.

Nicole stepped inside. She wore a robe and her hair was tousled.

"I slept in my clothes," she said, pulling a strand of hair back from her face. "But I don't remember the last time I slept that well." She looked at me, her eyes full of gratitude. "Thank you for last night."

"You're welcome."

She sat down on the corner of my bed.

"Are you going in to work?" I asked.

"No, I called in sick." She took a deep breath. "I have a big favor to ask of you."

"Whatever you need."

"Will you help me start my life over?"

I smiled. "Absolutely I will."

"Where do I begin?"

"We begin by bringing back Nicole."

She looked down for a moment. Then she

took a deep breath and stuck out her hand. "My name is Nicole Mitchell. It's nice to meet you."

"It's a pleasure meeting you, Nicole," I said. "Nicole needs a proper coming-out party. I say we start on Thanksgiving."

"Thanksgiving is tomorrow."

"Then we'll have to find people who don't have other plans. Do you know anyone who might be alone this Thanksgiving?"

She thought about it for a moment. "Bill," she said. "My landlord."

"What about Christine, your neighbor?"

"We can ask," she said.

"One more thing Nicole needs to do," I said. I looked at her seriously. "This won't be easy."

She took a deep breath, steeling herself to what I would say.

"Nicole had a son. A son she loved very much. Aiden needs to come back as well."

Her eyes watered. "How do I do that?"

"You talk about him. You put up pictures of him."

She wiped her eyes. "Okay."

I just looked at her for a moment, then said, "Welcome back, Nicole."

She clasped my hand. Then she stood. "I better go get dressed. We have a lot to do before tomorrow."

• • •

A half hour later Nicole and I sat down at the kitchen table to construct our shopping list. I held the pencil.

"All right," I said, "we need a turkey and stuffing."

"Write down bread crumbs, celery, and onions," Nicole said.

"Got it. And we need a can of cranberry sauce and we need yams . . ."

"I'm good at candied yams," Nicole said. "I make the diabetic-death kind with brown sugar and pecans."

"You are definitely in charge of yams."

"Write down pecan halves and butter," Nicole said.

"How about rolls?"

"I make awesome Parker House rolls."

"Fabulous. Turkey, stuffing, cranberry sauce, candied yams, rolls. Gravy. I can actually make turkey gravy," I said. "Do you have corn-starch?"

"Yes."

"How many should we prepare for?" I asked.

"At least three. Bill's coming."

"You already called him?"

"While you were showering. He was very excited."

"Okay, we'll plan on four. Worst case we'll have leftovers. I'll be in charge of the turkey, stuffing, and gravy. Oh, and eggnog. We need eggnog. Everyone loves eggnog."

"Not everyone," Nicole said.

"You don't like eggnog?"

"Diabetes aside, no. You can have my glass." I looked at her. "Really, Angel? You don't like eggnog?"

"Excuse me," she said.

"Eggnog is like the greatest drink ever."

"You called me Angel."

"No I didn't."

"Yes you did."

"Sorry. I won't do it again."

"Better not," she said.

I went back to my list. "Okay, we're still missing dessert."

"Pumpkin pie," Nicole said.

"Pumpkin pie and mashed potatoes. Do you say mashed or smashed?"

"Mashed. 'Smashed' sounds like they got run over by something."

I looked over the list. "I think we're ready."

"I'm not good at pies," she said.

"We can buy those."

"The bakery at Safeway is pretty good."

"Do you have potatoes?"

"No."

"Do you have enough milk?"

"I'll check." She opened the refrigerator. "Better get some more. Especially if you're

136

going to use some of it with your, gag, egg-nog."

"You don't need to disparage my eggnog," I said.

We put on our coats and started off. On our way out of the apartment we stopped and knocked on Christine's door. She answered wearing sweat pants and a Gonzaga basketball T-shirt. She looked surprised to see us.

"Angel," she said. "And Steven . . ."

"Alan," I corrected.

"Right, Alan. Sorry."

"And you can call me Nicole. Angel was just a nickname."

"Now I'm really confused," she said.

"It doesn't matter what you call us," I said. "We came to invite you to our Thanksgiving feast tomorrow at one."

A smile crossed her lips. "Really?"

"If you don't have other plans."

"I don't." To our surprise her eyes began to well up. "Sorry," she said, furtively wiping them. "I just thought I was going to spend the day alone. Thank you."

"Well, we'd love to have you."

"What can I bring?"

"Just yourself," Nicole said.

"I make really delicious mincemeat pies."

"*Good mincemeat* is an oxymoron," I said.

Nicole looked at me incredulously. "I can't believe you just said that."

"Sorry. But it looks like roadkill."

"That was even worse," she said.

"I know, mincemeat is an acquired taste," Christine said. "Don't worry, I also make an apple pie to die for and a pumpkin pie that's at least worth getting mugged for."

Nicole glanced over at me. "Worth getting mugged for."

"That must be some pie," I said. "I'm sold. You're in charge of pies. Then we'll see you tomorrow around one?"

"One. Thank you so much."

"Our pleasure," Nicole said.

I took Nicole's arm and we went off to the store.

They—"they" being the turkey experts—recommend a pound to a pound and a half of turkey per person, which meant a six-pound turkey should be plenty. But, since I'm partial to cold turkey leftovers, I selected an eight-pound bird. I also bought an entire gallon of eggnog, which Nicole thought was overkill. "No one's going to drink it but you," she said.

"Everyone loves eggnog," I said.

"Not everyone," she replied. "Some people have taste."

"Truce on the eggnog," I said.

"Truce," she said.

In addition to all the food we bought, we purchased other accoutrements of the season: scented candles, mistletoe, Christmas tree ornaments, and strings of Christmas tree lights. Through it all, Nicole was joyful.

As I was looking through the produce section, she brought an ornate silver picture frame to show me.

"What do you think?" she said. "I think it's pretty. It's sterling silver."

"It's beautiful," I said. "What's it for?"

"For Aiden," she said.

"Perfect," I said. "It's perfect."

Then she said, "I think I'll get two. I think Bill would like one as well."

A few minutes later I asked Nicole, "Do you have any Christmas music?"

"No."

"Do you have a stereo?"

"I have a CD player and an iPod."

"That will do." I purchased Christmas CDs by Burl Ives, Mitch Miller, and, of course, the Carpenters. As I showed the CDs to Nicole, I said, "Has anyone ever told you that you look like Karen Carpenter?"

"No."

"Really?"

"I don't look at all like Karen Carpenter. To begin with, I'm blond."

"Okay, so you're a blond version of Karen Carpenter."

"I don't look like her," she said, throwing her hands up in the air and walking away. I followed her with our shopping cart.

"I think you do," I said to myself.

I told Nicole to wait for me at the front door while I stopped at the video counter and picked up two movies. As I walked back, she tried to see the DVD cases I held in my hand.

"What movies did you get?"

"You'll see."

"Tell me," she laughed.

"You'll see," I said.

On the far corner of the strip mall was a Christmas tree lot.

"We need a tree," I said.

"I get to pick it out," she said. "It's my house."

"Fair enough," I replied.

Nicole found a nicely shaped Douglas fir about 6 feet high. The man selling the trees—his name was Maximilian (but just call me Max)— was so passionate about his trees that I was almost surprised he was willing to part with them. In addition to our Douglas fir, we left with a profusion of unrequested and useless information about our purchase, including:

- The Douglas fir is not really a fir tree.

- The Douglas fir is one of the few trees that naturally grow cone-shaped.
- The Douglas fir was named after David Douglas, some guy who studied the tree back in the 1800s.
- The Douglas fir was voted the number-two overall Christmas tree in America, second only to the South's Fraser fir, which, I assume, is a real fir tree.
- Max only sells Douglas firs.

Max tied the tree to the top of Nicole's Malibu and we drove home. After we had carried in all the food and put it away in the fridge, I grabbed a steak knife to cut the twine and went out to get the tree.

Our tree was gone.

I couldn't believe it. I shouted for Nicole from the porch and she came running outside.

"What?"

"Someone stole our tree."

"Right now?"

"Right off the car." I looked at her. "Who steals a Christmas tree?"

"Well, it *was* a Douglas fir," Nicole said, "the second-most-popular Christmas tree in the world."

I looked at her and grinned. "Do you think there's a black market for Douglas firs?"

"Huge market for stolen and kidnapped trees.

We'll probably get a ransom note any minute."

"Won't our thief be surprised when he learns that it's not even a real fir."

"Fake fir," Nicole said. "It would be like stealing a diamond ring and finding out it was only a zirconia."

"It would be just like that," I said.

We both burst out laughing. Then we went back to the store for another tree. Max gave us his "friends and family" discount of ten percent off our second one.

That evening we decorated the tree. After we finished, Nicole came out with the silver picture frame with a smiling photograph of her son. She set it on top of the television.

"He's a handsome kid," I said.

She smiled sadly. "Welcome back, son."

CHAPTER
Twenty-one

There can be no joy without gratitude.

Alan Christoffersen's diary

The next morning Nicole rapped on my door, then walked in. "Morning."

"Happy Thanksgiving," I said.

"Happy Thanksgiving to you. I called in sick to work again."

"How did that go?"

"My boss wasn't happy. I don't think she was buying it."

"Did you try to sound sick?"

"I did. But I'm not very good at it. I wonder if I'll get fired."

"I think you should just quit."

"Why? It's an important job."

"It is. But it depresses you."

"You're right, but I can't quit. I need the money. Besides, what do you do with a major in film studies? No, an *uncompleted* major in film studies."

"You could get a job at a theater. You could, like, sell popcorn."

She playfully hit me. "That will certainly pay the bills."

"We just need to find you a job with a little more positive energy." I looked over at the clock. "And we've got a lot of cooking to do. When should we put the turkey in?"

"Eight pounds, right?"

"Yes."

"It will probably take three hours. I'd allow three and a half to four, just in case."

"That would be right now," I said. "On it." I climbed out of bed.

Nicole began making rolls. She asked, "Were you planning on watching movies tonight?"

"Yeah."

"Will you tell me now what you got?"

"*It's a Wonderful Life . . .*"

"Good. A classic for Christmas. So why the mystery?"

". . . and *Citizen Kane*."

Her smile fell and she stopped kneading the dough. "Why did you choose that?"

"You spent months creating a timeline I want to derail."

She looked at me for a moment, then went back to her rolls. "You're very wise," she said.

"I think so," I said.

She threw a handful of flour at me.

Bill the landlord arrived early (his Old Spice arrived a few seconds earlier), a little before noon. He was dressed up as if he were going to church, wearing a hat, suspenders, and a red polka-dot bow tie. He brought a box of caramels with walnuts and a bottle of Cold Duck.

"Thank you for the invitation," he said to Nicole, taking off his hat as he entered. "I wish you'd reconsider moving." He turned to me. "Angel's been my best tenant."

"I've decided to stay," she said. "Just bring me a new lease."

"A new lease on life," he said.

She grinned. "You might say that. And you can call me Nicole."

He smiled. "I will be pleased to."

"We're still making dinner," she said. "Would you like to watch a football game on TV?"

"No, I don't care for that. If you don't mind, I'll just stay in here where the action is."

"We don't mind," she said.

"Would you like some eggnog?" I asked.

He waved his hand at me. "Don't drink the stuff, I'm lactose intolerant," he said.

"Another glass for you," Nicole whispered snidely.

Christine knocked on our door at the appointed hour. She wore a bright holiday sweater with Christmas bauble earrings. Her apartment door was wide open. She asked me, "Would you mind helping me bring over my pies?"

"Glad to," I said. "How many did you make?"

"Three. Apple, pumpkin, and . . . mincemeat."

"You made mincemeat just to spite me, didn't you?"

She smiled. "I like mincemeat." Then she added, "And to spite you."

"I'm not carrying the mincemeat," I said.

We carried back the pies. Nicole gasped as we entered. "Those look fabulous."

"Thank you. I love to bake, I just don't have anyone to bake for."

I looked at Nicole. "I think you two need to get together."

"We just did," she said.

"Hi, Bill," Christine said, walking into the kitchen.

"Hello, Chris," Bill said. "Is that mincemeat?"

"Yes it is."

"I love a good mincemeat."

Christine shot me a glance and Nicole grinned. "Looks like the mincemeat is beating out your eggnog," Nicole said.

I shrugged. "There's no accounting for taste in some people."

"My thought exactly," she replied.

"So how does a diabetic handle a Thanksgiving feast?" I asked.

"I'm not diabetic today."

"Really."

"Just kidding, but I'll use more insulin. I know it's not smart, but one day of the year . . . I'll live with it."

A half hour later we finished our preparations and sat down to eat.

"My, what a feast," Bill said, looking over the table. "I haven't seen a spread like this since June." We knew he wasn't talking about the month.

"I'd like to pray," Nicole said. She reached out and took Bill's hand and mine. Bill took Christine's hand and Christine took mine, completing the circle.

Nicole bowed her head. "Dear Father, I am grateful this day for my friends and for Alan and his care. We are grateful for this food and for so much to be grateful for. We ask a blessing on those without and to be led to help them. Also, we are grateful for those who are missing from our lives. Amen."

"Amen," I said.

"Amen," Bill and Christine said.

"Before we eat," Nicole said, "I would like to take a moment and say something, if that's all right."

"Of course," Bill said. "Speech, speech."

"Well, it's not really a speech," she said. "In better days my family used to always say one

147

thing we were grateful for before we could eat. I'd like to do the same."

We all agreed.

"Alan, would you start?"

I looked around the table as all eyes turned to me. "Sure." I sat up a little. "This is my first holiday without McKale. If you had asked me a year ago what I was most grateful for, I would have said McKale. If you asked me today, I'd say the same thing. I guess sometimes we're lucky to have someone to miss so much."

Nicole smiled sadly.

"I'm grateful to be here today with all of you, for this food and home. I'm grateful to be feeling so much better. Most of all, I'm grateful for Nicole, for taking care of me and encouraging me through it all. I don't know how I would have made it without her. That's it," I said.

Bill nodded thoughtfully.

"I'll go," Christine said, turning to Nicole. "I'm grateful that you invited me to have dinner with you. I thought it was going to be another crummy Thanksgiving alone. Money's kind of tight, so I won't be flying home until school gets out. So I'm grateful to have friends to make me feel thankful."

"Amen," Nicole said.

"How about you, Bill?" I said.

He looked down at his plate as he gathered his thoughts. Then he looked up at all of us, his eyes eventually landing on Nicole. "Since I lost my June, I've been pretty lonely. So I guess I'm a bit like Christine—I thought this was going to be another crummy day alone with my memories. Thank God there are people like you, Nicole, who would include an old man in your festivities."

"It's been my pleasure, Bill," Nicole said. She took a deep breath. "I guess it's my turn. Last Thanksgiving I was in a hospital bed, alone and going through the most difficult experience of my life. This day I am grateful for all of you. You've said such kind things. You don't know how much it means to me. I'm especially grateful that Alan came into my life at this time." She took my hand. "I thought I went to the hospital to help you. I didn't realize that it was for me. Thank you for not leaving me like everyone else did. Thank you for caring."

I looked deeply into her eyes. She continued. "Today I am mostly grateful for life. It seems we've all had tough years lately. I don't know about you, Christine, but the three of us have all lost someone we've loved. But as hard as the last few years have been, I'm still grateful for them. I'm grateful for the good days I've had. There haven't been too many of them lately, but I have hope that there will be more to come. I hope that's true for all of us."

Christine's eyes were beaming and Bill

looked like he was getting emotional or about to. I raised my glass of eggnog. "Here, here."

Everyone else raised their glasses and we toasted.

"Now let's eat before we all die of hunger," Nicole said.

I stood to serve the turkey and we began dishing out the food.

"Angel, would you please pass me the mashed potatoes?" Christine asked.

"She's going by Nicole, now," Bill said.

"Oh right. Sorry."

"Angel was a nickname," Nicole said. "But I'm through with it."

I looked at her proudly.

The meal was delicious and the conversation kept up, covering a broad range of topics from the origin of mincemeat to where we were when the Space Shuttle exploded.

The sum of the day was truly greater than its parts. The four of us loners talked and laughed like old friends, like we hadn't a care in the world. Maybe, for that moment, we didn't.

We all did the dishes, even Bill, who claimed that under his wife's regime, KP was his job. When the kitchen was clean, Bill hugged Nicole. "Thank you."

"You're not staying for the movie?"

"No, I think I'll just retire. But thank you for

everything. It was a wonderful meal. I had a most enjoyable time."

"You're very welcome," Nicole said. "We should get together again."

His face lit. "I'd enjoy that immensely."

The three of us watched *It's a Wonderful Life.* Christine spent most of the evening with us but left before the movie was over. She hugged both of us and set a date to go out with Nicole.

Jimmy Stewart was on his knees begging for life when there was a knock at the door. Nicole stood. "Christine must have forgotten something."

"I'll pause the movie," I said.

"That's okay. I've already seen it a million times."

I glanced over as she opened the door. I couldn't see who was in the hall, but I heard a man's voice. Nicole said something then glanced back at me. "Alan, it's for you."

"For me?"

She took a couple steps toward me. "It's your father."

CHAPTER
Twenty-two

My father came. No matter what he said, his search for me spoke louder.

Alan Christoffersen's diary

I looked at Nicole in disbelief. "My father?"
She nodded.
I got up from the couch and walked to the door. My father stood in the hallway wearing his Los Angeles Lakers windbreaker. For a moment we just looked at each other. Then he stepped forward and threw his arms around me.
"Son."
My father rarely hugged me and never in front of others, so it felt unnatural. He held me for nearly a minute before he released me, stepping back, his hands still on my shoulders. Only then did I see that his eyes were red.
"Thank God you're okay. When I learned that you had been stabbed . . ." He stopped, affected by emotion. He wiped his eyes with the back of one hand. "Are you okay?"
"Much better than I was four weeks ago," I said, my mind swimming with questions. "How did you find me?"

"Falene called me."

His reply only raised more questions. Falene was my assistant at Madgic, my former advertising firm and the only employee who had remained loyal to me when Kyle stole the agency. After McKale's death, when I decided to shut everything down, I had asked Falene to liquidate everything I owned and put the receipts in an account for me. I knew she had been busy—evidenced by the growing bank account—but I hadn't spoken to her since I left Seattle.

"How did Falene know where I was?"

"She didn't. She had been tracking your walk by your credit card transactions until they stopped just outside of Spokane. She became worried that something had happened to you, and she called me to see if I'd heard from you.

"I've got to tell you, when she told me that you were walking across the country, you could have knocked me over with a feather. I didn't even know you had left Seattle."

"I'm sorry, I should have told you." The truth was, my father and I had never been close, I hadn't even thought to call him.

"After her call, the first call I made was to the Spokane Police Department. They told me that you had been assaulted and taken to the hospital. I called over there, but no one could answer my questions about where you were, so I flew up here and nosed around until I found someone who knew where you were."

"Norma," I said.

"A nurse, about yea high, blond." He held his hand out horizontally from his chest.

"That's her," I said. I stepped back a little. "Come inside, let's talk."

My father stepped inside. Nicole had turned off the DVD and was standing near the couch watching us.

"Dad, this is my friend Nicole. She offered to take me in when the hospital released me."

Nicole walked over to us, shaking my father's hand. "It's a pleasure to meet you, Mr. Christoffersen. Please, sit down."

"Thank you."

My father walked over to the couch and sat. I shut the door behind him and sat down on the far end of the sofa. "Join us," I said to Nicole.

She sat.

"Your name is Nicole?" my father asked. "I was told my son had gone home with a woman named Angel."

"Angel's my nickname," she said.

He nodded. "Well, Nicole, I want to thank you for taking care of my son."

"It's been my pleasure. In fact, you might say that he's been taking care of me."

My father turned back to me. "Falene said that you were walking to Key West, Florida."

154

"That's the plan."

He looked down for a moment as if trying to process my reply. "I don't even know what to say to that. You told me that your business was struggling a bit, but you didn't tell me it had gone under and you'd lost your home."

"Things fell apart pretty quickly."

He nodded. "I'm just glad you're alive. You're not going to keep walking now, are you?"

"As soon as the weather permits. I'm grounded here until spring."

His forehead creased. "Could I talk you out of it?"

I shook my head. "No."

"Could I bribe you out of it?"

"No."

He sat back. "It's dangerous out there."

"That's for sure," Nicole said.

After a minute my father asked Nicole, "How is it that you two know each other?"

Nicole said, "Serendipity, really. We met outside a town about a hundred miles from here when Alan stopped to fix my tire. The police called me after he was attacked."

"That is serendipitous. Did the police catch the hoodlums?"

"Yes," I said. "As far as I know they're in jail. The kid who stabbed me is dead."

My dad looked at me with a peculiar expression I'd never seen on his face before—a hybrid between shock and admiration. "You killed him?"

"No, I was unconscious. The kid attacked the men who saved me and they shot him. He died in the same hospital I was in."

My father just shook his head. "Where are the parents these days?"

Nicole leaned forward. "Mr. Christoffersen . . ."

"Bob," he said. "Call me Bob."

"Have you eaten?"

"I had a burger earlier."

"That's not acceptable on Thanksgiving Day. We have a complete Thanksgiving feast in the refrigerator. May I put something together for you?"

"If it's not too much trouble."

"No trouble at all. You two just stay in here and catch up," she said, running off to the kitchen.

"Nice gal," my father said after she was gone.

"Yes she is."

My father clasped his hands together in his lap. "When Falene told me you lost the house . . ." He looked up at me. "Why didn't you call me? I could have helped."

"I was kind of a wreck."

"That and you didn't feel like you could."

I looked down. "I guess not."

"I'm sorry for that. I truly am."

● ● ●

Ten minutes later Nicole walked back in. "Dinner's ready."

My father smiled and stood. I followed him into the kitchen. The table was laid out with platters and a single dinner plate with utensils.

"Now that's a feast," my father said.

My father was never a big eater, but he surprised me, eating large portions and seconds of everything. I sat down next to him and ate slices of cold turkey breast sandwiched between rolls.

"How long are you in town?" Nicole asked.

"I was prepared to stay as long as I needed to." He looked at me. "But now that I've found my son, I'll probably leave tomorrow."

"Why don't you stay the weekend?" I asked. "It would be nice having you around."

I could see that he appreciated my offer. "I'd like that."

"Where are you staying?" Nicole asked.

"Over at the airport Ramada."

"You could stay here," she offered. "I'll sleep on the couch."

"No, no. I'm fine. All my stuff's over there and it's not much of a drive to get here."

"Have you had enough to eat?"

"I've had enough for a small village. You don't have any eggnog do you?"

Nicole smiled. "Plenty. I'll pour you a glass."

"I dilute it with milk, half and half."

"Like father, like son," she said.

When my father had finished eating, he thanked Nicole profusely. Then I walked with him out to his rental car. He started the car, turned on its defroster and wipers, then climbed out as it warmed.

"Thank you for coming," I said.

"Of course I came." He stood in the cold, his breath freezing before him. "I haven't had a decent night's sleep since Falene called. So if it's all right by you, I think I'm going to sleep in tomorrow."

"Sounds good."

He nodded. "I'll see you sometime after noon. Good night, son."

"Night, Dad."

He opened the door and then stopped. "That Falene's a nice gal. You better give her a call. She was beside herself with worry."

"I'll call her tonight."

"She'll be glad." He climbed inside the car, then slowly pulled away from the curb. Nicole met me in the doorway.

"I can't believe he came," I said.

"And he likes eggnog."

"He does like eggnog."

"Glad someone does," she said. "We've still got a whole gallon of it in there."

CHAPTER
Twenty-three

Developing a friendship is like feeding
squirrels at the park. At first it's all
grab and go. But with gentle motion,
time and consistency, soon
they're eating from your hand.

Alan Christoffersen's diary

I borrowed Nicole's phone to call Falene. Her
phone rang six times before it went to voice mail.
I hung up without leaving a message, then
redialed the number. I remembered that Falene
rarely answered numbers she didn't know but
sometimes did if the caller was persistent. The
phone rang awhile again and I was about to
hang up when she answered. "Hello."

"Falene, it's Alan."

Silence.

"Are you there?" I asked.

"Where have you been?"

I wasn't sure if the question was rhetorical or
if she really wanted an answer. "I'm in
Spokane."

"You're in Spokane," she said, her voice rising.
"And I'm over here worried to death. Your
father is out looking for you, I've been calling

all the hospitals from here to Denver. For all I knew you were lying on the side of some road dead. Of all the selfish—"

"Falene—"

"I'm not done. You couldn't take just five minutes and call me? I'm not worth just five minutes of your time? Here I've been killing myself liquidating everything, taking crap from the vendors and trying to answer these questions by—"

"Falene, I'm sorry. You're right, I've been selfish."

"No, you're *incredibly* selfish. You're the most selfish, insensitive—"

"Falene. Just stop."

Surprisingly, she did, though she was still breathing heavily.

"Thank you," I said.

She breathed out in exasperation. "Where are you?"

"I'm in Spokane," I repeated.

"Your father's in Spokane right now looking for you."

"He found me."

"He said you'd been stabbed. Is it true?"

"I was jumped by a gang. I was stabbed three times."

"Where?"

"Just outside Spokane."

"I mean, where on your body?"

"In the stomach. Fortunately, he missed all my vital organs."

"Are you okay?"

"It took a few weeks before I could walk again, but I've mostly recovered."

She breathed out slowly. "I'm sorry I got so mad. I've been terrified for the last three weeks. I was worried that something bad had happened and I was right."

"I'm sorry I didn't call. I'm not saying it's an excuse, but I don't have my cell phone anymore, so I don't think about it."

"What happened to your cell phone?"

"I threw it in a lake."

She didn't ask why.

"I didn't know that you had been following me," I said.

"Of course I've been following you."

"How are you doing?" I asked.

"I'm okay. I've finished liquidating all the furniture from the office. About half the furniture from your home is still at the consignment shop. There's around forty-six thousand in the account. I hope it's okay, but I took four thousand for my salary and to pay my brother for helping me."

"I offered you half of what you brought in."

"I know, but that was too much. I just needed a little. Besides, I got another job. I'm now the office manager at Tiffany's Modeling. I've tripled my modeling gigs and I get my head shots for free."

"I'm glad that's working out."

"You know, being at Tiffany's, I see a lot of the other agency guys we used to compete with. They ask about you all the time."

"What do you tell them?"

"I tell them that you took a job with BBDO in the U.K."

I laughed. "Why don't you just tell them the truth?"

"It's none of their business. Yesterday, I saw Jason Stacey from Sixty-Second. He told me that Kyle's losing clients almost as fast as his hair and that he and Ralph parted ways. Ralph took a job with some credit union doing in-house graphic design."

"That didn't last long," I said. Kyle had been my partner at Madgic. While I was caring for McKale, he had covertly started his own advertising agency, stolen my clients and talked Ralph, my head of graphic design, into coming on as his partner. I had hired and trained Ralph myself, so his betrayal was especially hard on me. "It's only been about two months."

"Apparently, cheaters don't prosper. In fact you'll never guess who I got a call from the other day. Phil Wathen."

The name sent a pang through my body. Phil was a real estate developer, and it was his $6 million account I was pitching when I learned of McKale's accident.

"What did Phil have to say?"

"He wanted to know if you'd consider taking him back as a client. I guess Kyle's not keeping him happy either."

"Karma sucks," I said.

She laughed. "I miss you."

"I miss you too."

"I have some tax papers I need signed, where should I send them?"

"I'm staying at a friend's house. You could send the documents here."

"How about if I just brought them?"

Her offer surprised me. "You don't need to go to that much trouble."

"It's no trouble. Besides, I have the week between Christmas and New Year's off, I'd love to see you."

"I'd like that," I said.

"Then I'll come." She sighed. "I better let you go. Have a happy Thanksgiving."

"Happy Thanksgiving to you," I said.

"It is now," she replied.

I hung up the phone. I had forgotten how good it was to talk to her.

CHAPTER
Twenty-four

We watched Citizen Kane. I'm
pleased to witness that, in this instance,
the movie ended entirely different
than it was supposed to.

Alan Christoffersen's diary

Long conversations (and most short ones) were
not a part of my experience growing up with my
father, so I wondered what we would talk about
that afternoon. My worries were in vain. My
father arrived around noon and immediately
started poking around Nicole's house for something to repair, which is his favorite pastime. His
discoveries necessitated two trips to Home
Depot. He repaired a leaky faucet, weather-
stripped two windows, and replaced a refrigerator bulb before he sat down with me to watch
the Alabama-Auburn game.

Nicole came home from work at her usual hour.
We ate a dinner of Thanksgiving leftovers, then
my dad and I decided to meet at noon for lunch
the next day.

After he left, Nicole and I popped some corn,
then sat down and watched *Citizen Kane*.

When it was over, Nicole said, "Did you know

that *Citizen Kane* was about William Randolph Hearst? He owned dozens of newspapers, and when the movie came out, he not only banned them from mentioning the film, but he threatened to cut advertising from any movie theater that played it."

"Can't say that I blame him," I said.

"It does make him look pretty ruthless. The film never did well at the box office. In the end, the film destroyed both men—Hearst and Welles."

"How do you know all this?"

"Remember, I'm a film major."

"Oh yeah."

"That was also true of *It's a Wonderful Life*."

"Hearst didn't like it?"

She laughed. "No, it also bombed at the box office. People thought it was just too depressing."

I thought about this. "But we like it now."

She smiled. "We most certainly do."

CHAPTER
Twenty-five

There are two kinds of people.
Those who climb mountains and
those who sit in the shadow of the
mountains and critique the climbers.

Alan Christoffersen's diary

True to his nature, my father arrived at the house the next day precisely five minutes before twelve. "If you're not five minutes early, you're late," he always said, and he was as punctual as he was thrifty—which would impress you if you knew how thrifty he really was.

Even though it was lunchtime, we went to the IHOP for pancakes. IHOP was a tradition for me. Whenever we pulled an all-nighter at the agency, we'd all end up at IHOP, sometimes at three in the morning.

We both ordered a tall stack of pancakes—him buckwheat, me blueberry. When we'd gotten our meals, he asked, "How are you dealing with McKale?"

"I have my moments."

He looked at me knowingly. "You know, after your mother died, some of my colleagues tried to get me to start dating, but I didn't. That was a mistake."

"I'm not interested in dating right now," I said.

"I'm not saying you should be, it's too early. But I hope you would someday consider it."

"Why didn't you?"

"Well, there are the lies we tell ourselves and then there's the truth. I told myself that I didn't want to confuse you by bringing home a strange woman. But the truth was, I was afraid of throwing the dice again. I was always shy, so your mother was the only woman I had ever dated. I got lucky with her. I didn't think a man should hope to get that lucky twice in one lifetime." My father poured maple syrup on his pancakes. "I'm just saying, don't be a coward like me. Life is short. You should find love when and where you can."

I was surprised to hear this from him. "You're no coward."

"Sure I am. Cowards always hide behind bravado or stoicism. It takes courage to show emotion." He took a bite of pancake. "Anyway, I've been thinking a lot about your walk. How'd you come up with your destination?"

"It was the furthest point on the map."

He nodded as if he understood. "Have you ever been to Key West?"

"No."

"Me neither," he said. "Anyway, I'm not against it—your walking there."

"You've changed your mind?"

"I guess it was never really set. When I first heard, I didn't know why you'd want to do such a crazy thing, but the more I thought about it, the more sense it made. I think I know why you need to walk."

I was curious to hear his reasoning, especially since I wasn't totally sure myself. "Why?"

"When I was twenty-something I read this book written by a German psychiatrist. He was a survivor of the Auschwitz concentration camp.

"That book had a profound effect on me. Something that he said has always stuck with me. Maybe this is just my interpretation, but basically he wrote that when a man loses his vision of the future he dies.

"There's a lot of talk these days about living in the now, but if you don't have a future, there is no now. You see it all the time. Men retire from their jobs and a few months later the paper runs their obituary.

"I'll be honest with you, when I lost your mother, there were days I wanted to put a gun to my head. But I still had you. And I had my job and my buddies at the Rotary. All that kept me from derailing.

"But you weren't so fortunate. You lost it all. Lesser men have given up under such circumstances. But you found something to keep you going. I think that's admirable. I think it's more than that, I think it's manly."

That may have been the greatest accolade I had ever received from my father. Almost instinctively, I tried to deflect it. "I almost gave up."

"*Almost* has no consequence in this world. None whatsoever. You didn't give up, that's all that matters." He set down his fork and leaned forward. "Do you know why men climb mountains?"

I looked at him blankly. "Because they're there?"

"Because the valley is for cemeteries. Sometimes, when tragedy strikes, people give up hope that they can expect anything more from life, when the real quest is finding out what life expects from them. Does this make any sense?"

"It makes sense," I said.

"So, my CPA-trained mind must ask, do you have the financial means to carry out your trek?"

"I think so. I have about forty-six thousand dollars."

"As long as you don't stay at the Four Seasons, that should get you through. You're not carrying all that money with you."

"No. I use a credit card and ATM machines. Falene liquidated all our assets and put it in an account."

"I don't like the ATM fees," he said, sounding more accountant than father, "but I suppose it can't be avoided. The account is interest-bearing, I presume."

"I really don't know."

He frowned. He never understood why I was so lax about such things. "Well, if, for any reason you come up short, you come to me. It may surprise you, but I've got quite a nest egg put away."

"It doesn't surprise me at all. You're a hard worker and the most frugal person I've ever met. If I were more like you, I wouldn't be in such a mess."

"If you were more like me, you'd be a bored, unhappy old man."

I was surprised by his comment.

"I know I've come down on you more than a few times for being irresponsible with your money, but I'm being honest with you now—a part of me admires that about you. You and McKale lived. You had fun. And now you have those memories. I didn't, and you and your mom suffered because of it. I suffered because of it."

"We had good times," I said.

"Course we did, but they were few and far between. I put things off with your mother that I regret to this day. One Christmas she wanted to go to Italy more than anything. She begged me to go. She said she didn't want another thing for Christmas or her birthday, she said she'd cut coupons, get a side job and save her dimes. She even had a sitter lined up for you." He shook his head. "Idiot I was, I told her 'no.' 'Too expensive,' I said. 'A waste of money.' Instead we drove to Yellowstone Park."

"I remember that trip to Yellowstone," I said. "I have fond memories of it. Didn't Mom want to go?"

"You wouldn't know it if she didn't, but I knew that her heart was set on Italy." Suddenly, my father's eyes welled up with tears. "I didn't know that would be our last vacation together." He cleared his throat. "The kicker is, we had the money—even back then. I saved up all this money for retirement and for what? To give it to someone else? I live alone and still go in to work every day. I'll never use the half of it, just leave it to you. I should just give it all to you now, you'd know what to do with it."

"I'd just lose it," I said. "At least I would have."

"In the end, we all lose it. Remember that. In the end, we own nothing."

It struck me odd hearing this from a man who had spent his career counseling people on how to keep their money. I didn't know if my father had changed or if I'd just never seen this side of him. Probably both.

We finished our pancakes, then my father drove me back to Nicole's. Idling at the curb, he asked in his direct, pragmatic way, "Anything else we need to talk about?"

"No."

"Then I'll go home tomorrow."

"Okay," I said.

"It's settled," he said.

I got out of the car. As I started up the walk, he rolled down the window. "Son."

I turned back. "Yes?"

"I love you."

I looked at him for a few seconds, then said, "I know. Me too."

He put the car in gear and drove away.

CHAPTER
Twenty-six

Funny how we can wait so many
years to hear so few words.

Alan Christoffersen's diary

My father came by to see me once more before
he left. He was wearing his Lakers windbreaker
again, with a Lakers cap. He came inside the
building but not Nicole's apartment.

"It was good seeing you, son."

"Thanks for coming."

"Where's Angel? I'd like to say goodbye."

"Nicole," I corrected. "She's inside." I called to
Nicole and she walked out.

"I want to thank you for taking care of my
son," he said.

"My pleasure. And thank you for all the things
you fixed around here."

"I like puttering around. If there's ever anything I can do for you, just call."

"Thank you," she said.

They looked at each other for a moment, then
Nicole stuck out her hand. "Travel safe."

"Thank you."

He put his hand on my shoulder. "Come out to
the car with me."

I followed him out. When we were at the curb, my father said, "Three things I ask of you. First, take this." He handed me a small cell phone, the inexpensive kind they give you when you open a new cell phone account. "Just for emergencies. No one needs to know the number and you can keep it turned off. I won't call you, but you call now and then. I don't mean daily, but every couple of weeks just to let me know you're okay.

"Second, if you need help, you come to me. I want you to promise me that."

"I promise," I said, and I actually meant it.

"Good, good. Third." He reached into the car's trunk and brought out a small bag. "Here's the charger for your cell phone. And here's something else you'll need."

I looked at what he was handing me. "A handgun?"

"Nine-millimeter. The safety's on, clip is empty."

I pushed it back to him. "I don't do guns."

"If you're going to live on the road, you better have it. You didn't even get out of Washington without almost getting killed. You've got thousands of miles to go and I'm betting you'll be walking through places a whole lot tougher than Spokane."

I looked at the gun skeptically. "I don't know."

"If you won't do it for yourself, do it for me. For my peace of mind."

"Is it even legal?"

"It's registered in my name. But I'm guessing your next mugger won't care much."

I balanced the piece in my hand. After a moment I said, "All right."

"Good. Don't forget the shells. One box should be ample." He wiped his nose with the back of his hand. "Are you going through Colorado?"

"I haven't decided."

"If you do, drop by and see the Laidlaws. I haven't seen them in years."

"If I'm in the neighborhood I'll be sure to do that."

He stepped forward and hugged me. "Take care of yourself. I'm glad you're my boy."

All I could say was "Thanks." I'd wanted to hear that for the longest time.

CHAPTER
Twenty-seven

Then pealed the bells more loud and deep;
"God is not dead, nor doth He sleep."
—Longfellow

Alan Christoffersen's diary

My mother often said that the shortest path to healing was to heal someone else. I never knew how right she was. In caring for Nicole I had almost forgotten my own loss and grief. By all rights that holiday season should have been despairing, or at least melancholy, and, of course, I had those moments, but they didn't define the season. I didn't forget McKale—that would have been impossible. I just found a different side of my loss, focusing more on the sweetness of what was than the bitterness of what wasn't.

Nicole also seemed different, as if reclaiming her name had changed everything else about her life. For the first time since I came home with her, she stopped talking about the horrors she encountered on her job and started talking about the positive ones, like the work the police were doing to help kids during the holiday season or the people who rescued complete strangers at personal risk to themselves.

We weren't watching movies from her list anymore, just a few Christmas ones—*Miracle on 34th Street*, *White Christmas*, and *A Charlie Brown Christmas*—but we kept busy, making the most of the holiday.

We went to a stage production of *A Christmas Carol*, the planetarium's presentation of *The Star of Bethlehem*, and toured the *Christmas Tree Elegance* presentation in downtown Spokane at the Davenport Hotel.

One Saturday we drove across the border into Coeur d'Alene, Idaho, for their remarkable holiday light show: more than a million and a half lights over the lake.

With the exception of our escapade into Coeur d'Alene, we brought Bill (and his Old Spice) along with us to almost everything, including a Christmas singalong at the neighboring Montessori. It was fun watching how happy he was to be included, and I realized that what I was doing for Nicole, she was doing for Bill.

Through it all there was something remarkably seductive about denying the dwindling candle of Nicole and my allotted time together and believing in something more permanent. That level of denial might sound peculiar, but, on some level, we all do that every day.

CHAPTER
Twenty-eight

The giving of a Christmas fruitcake
has been passed down from
generation to generation to
generation. That's because
nobody wanted it.

Alan Christoffersen's diary

Christmas Eve. Christine had flown home to
Portland to spend Christmas with her family, but
Bill joined us. The three of us had a nice ham
dinner with scalloped potatoes, asparagus, and a
fruit salad. Bill brought a fruitcake, which
reminded me of what Johnny Carson had to say
about fruitcakes. "There's only been one fruitcake
ever made—and every Christmas it gets passed
around the world."

After dinner we exchanged our gifts. I gave
Nicole the complete set of Alfred Hitchcock
movies and a year's supply of microwave
popcorn. I gave Bill a bottle of Old Spice. He
caressed the bottle as if it were a fine wine.
"How did you know I like this?" he asked.

"Lucky guess," I said.

Nicole gave him the silver picture frame.

"I think it's the most beautiful picture frame I've ever seen," he said.

"I thought you could put a picture of June in it."

His eyes welled up with tears and his chin began to quiver a little. All he could say was "Thank you."

Nicole gave me something less sentimental— a pair of Nike walking shoes and seven pairs of wool athletic socks.

The snow was falling gently, casting the world in a serene, peaceful air as we walked Bill out to his car. He shook my hand, then turned to Nicole and embraced her tightly. "Thank you, my dear. Your friendship means more to me than I could ever tell you. God bless you."

"God bless you, Bill. And Merry Christmas. Don't forget we have brunch tomorrow. We'll pick you up around eleven."

"I won't eat a thing before."

"And don't forget our wild New Year's Eve party. I fully expect to see you wearing a lamp shade before the night's through."

He chuckled heartily. "Oh, that would be a sight. I'll be there, unless, of course, I'm too tired. You youngsters keep me up too late. I haven't stayed up this late for years."

"It's good for you," Nicole said.

"I'll take your word for it." He leaned forward and kissed her on the cheek. "Good night, my dear."

As he drove off, Nicole said, "He's a sweet old guy."

"I don't think you have any idea how much you mean to him," I said.

"It's mutual," she said, smiling. She took my hand. "I have a gift for you."

"You already gave me a gift."

"No, that was a necessity."

Back inside, she told me to sit on the couch as she ran into her bedroom. The Christmas tree lit the front room, its blinking lights flashing on and off in syncopation.

She returned a few seconds later with a package. "Okay, so you're both easy and difficult to shop for. On the one hand, what do you give a man who has nothing?"

"Anything," I said.

"Exactly. On the other hand, what do you give a man who carries his home on his back?" Her expression turned softer. "Or the man who saved your life?" She handed me the box. "Anyway, I hope you like it."

I peeled back the paper to expose a crushed velvet jewelry box. I opened the lid. Inside was a St. Christopher medallion.

"St. Christopher is the patron saint of travelers," she said. "Do you like it?"

I lifted the white gold medallion by its chain. "It's beautiful." I unclasped the chain and put it around my neck. The pendant fell to the top of my chest.

"I hope you'll think of me every time you feel it against your skin."

I leaned over and kissed her cheek.

Suddenly, she said, "Hey, how about some eggnog?"

"You'll actually join me in a glass?"

"No, but I'll watch."

I laughed. "Fair enough."

CHAPTER
Twenty-nine

The greatest gift I received this
Christmas was peace.

Alan Christoffersen's diary

Christmas Day was joyous and relaxed. Just before noon we picked up Bill, then drove downtown for Christmas brunch at the Davenport, which Bill insisted on paying for. "I'm starting to feel like a charity case," he said.

After the meal we came back to the apartment and spent the rest of the day playing card games until Bill got tired and we drove him home.

On the way back Nicole asked, "How was your Christmas?"

"It was great." I looked at her and smiled. "That's kind of amazing, isn't it? I thought I'd be suicidal by now. Instead, I feel peace."

As she pondered my words, a grin spread across her face. "May I tell you something awful?"

I looked at her curiously. "What's that?"

"I'm glad you got stabbed." She covered her mouth with her hand.

I just looked at her, then burst out laughing. "Me too."

The next morning Nicole had to go back to work. I got in my walking, which I had been less than diligent about through the holidays. I walked seven miles and I could feel it in my legs. I came back and showered, then spent the rest of the day at home waiting for Falene.

Falene arrived around two-thirty, driving a fire engine red BMW. I walked outside and waved her down. She climbed out of the car wearing Chanel sunglasses and a form-fitting, one-piece sweater-dress.

"Alan," she shouted.

"Hey."

She bounded up the walk to me and we embraced.

"Aren't you a sight for sore eyes," she said, kissing my cheek. "I've missed you."

"I've missed you too," I said. "Have you had lunch?"

"I've just been mainlining Diet Cokes."

"As usual. Want to go get a burger?"

"Oh yes, real food. Please." She handed me her keys. "You drive."

We drove to a Wendy's where I got a salad and she got a double cheeseburger, giant fries, and a chocolate Frosty with a Diet Coke to counter it.

"I get so sick of starving myself," she said, "sometimes I've just got to binge."

"How's Seattle?" I asked, stealing one of her fries.

"Rain," she said. "And more rain, and then some more."

"You gotta love that rain. Speaking of storms, tell me more about Ralph and Kyle."

Falene grinned. "Did you really come up with that segue on the fly?"

"Of course."

"You're still brilliant. Well, I told you they split. But it gets better," she said. "Or worse, depending on whose side you're on. Ralph's wife finally found out he was cheating."

"I might have had something to do with that," I said.

"You told his wife?"

"I ran into Ralph and Cheryl up at Stevens Pass. They didn't recognize me since I had a beard and glasses, but I made a comment to him about cheaters."

She shook her head. "Serves him right, the weasel. Ralph was nothing until you brought him in, and then he plots behind your back to steal your agency."

"What about Kyle?"

"You know how he always bragged that he could talk his way out of anything?"

"Yes."

"Well, apparently there comes a time when people actually expect results. Let's face it, everything brilliant that ever came out of Madgic was yours. They may have stolen your clients and the awards off the wall, but they can't take your creativity. It was only a matter of time before the wheels fell off." She took a bite of her Frosty. "I've got to tell you, you've walked a long way. Just driving here made me tired."

"I've just begun."

"Are you really going to walk the whole way?"

"I'm still planning on it."

"So, what was it like being stabbed?"

"It hurt."

A grin crossed her face. "I figured that much. Does it still hurt?"

"No. There's a little numbness, but nothing compared to what it was."

"May I see?"

"Sure." I lifted my shirt to show her the wounds. I had removed the bandages several weeks earlier, so all that was left were three fresh scars. She grimaced. "You poor baby. You should have stayed with me."

"I had to leave Seattle."

Just then a guy walked by staring at Falene as if his eyes were caught in a tractor beam. I forgot that this is how it was whenever I was with her. She didn't even notice it anymore.

"Where did you meet Nicole?" she asked.

"I came across her while I was walking. She had a flat tire and I stopped to help her."

"Always the good Samaritan, aren't you?"

"Not always."

"Next time something happens, you call me."

"I promise the next time I'm stabbed, I'll call you first."

She grinned.

"How is the liquidation of my estate going?"

"Well. I think we'll probably bring in another twenty thousand on furniture before we're done."

"I can't thank you enough for all you've done."

"You can start by keeping in touch. Every week."

"I promise."

". . . and when you arrive in Key West, I want to be there."

I wasn't sure how to respond to her request. "Let me think about it."

"Okay," she said, "you think about it."

Falene and I sat and talked for nearly two and a half hours, long after the ice had melted in her Coke and the sun had started to set. Afterward we drove downtown to look at the lights.

Nicole's car was out front when we arrived home. I pulled up behind her car and we got out. I led Falene up to the house and opened the apartment door. "Nicole," I shouted. "We're home."

Nicole walked into the front room from the hallway.

"Nicole," I said, "this is Falene."

"Hi," Nicole said, extending her hand. "It's a pleasure to meet you."

"It's my pleasure," Falene said.

"We're going to get Falene checked into a hotel, then we're headed out to dinner," I said. "Want to come?"

"No, I'm sure you two have a lot to catch up on."

"We've plenty of time for that," I said. "Come on."

"Yes, come," Falene said. "It will be fun."

"Actually," she said, "I already have a date."

I looked at her with surprise. "Really? With who?"

"Bill. We're going to see the ice sculptures at Candlelight Park."

"How romantic," Falene said.

I started laughing. "Bill's her landlord. He's like ninety."

"Oh?" Falene said. "You can't be romantic at ninety?"

Nicole smiled. "Exactly. Besides, he's only eighty-seven," she said lightly. "And it will be romantic. Bill's a real gentleman."

"My apologies," I said. "Have a good time."

Falene and I walked out to the curb. I opened the door for her, then walked around to my door. I looked back once more. Nicole was still standing at the window watching us. She waved. I waved back then got in and we drove off to dinner.

CHAPTER
Thirty

Old friends are memories personified.

Alan Christoffersen's diary

Falene checked herself into the Davenport Hotel, and we decided to eat at the Palm Court Grill in the hotel's lobby. The restaurant was quiet, and we sat in the corner away from everyone else, which was good since we laughed so much.

It was nice to laugh again. I think Falene remembered every amusing anecdote from our time together, including my April Fools campaign for KBOX 107.9 radio. I had created a billboard campaign dealing with their radio hosts' body parts, such as:

MARK HAS AN *EAR* FOR THE HITS

The words were positioned next to an enlarged picture of Mark's ear. There was also:

DANNY *KNOWS* YOUR FAVORITE SONGS

The words appeared next to a picture of

Danny's nose. Yeah, it wasn't my best campaign, but it did the job.

Since the campaign was scheduled to start on April Fools Day, as a joke I had the printer change the lettering on one of Danny's signs, which I personally brought down to the station. He sat quietly as I unveiled the board. Next to a very extreme close-up of his nose were the words:

DANNY *PICKS* YOUR FAVORITES

His expression was priceless. I then told him that I had made an executive decision and changed all thirty exposures at the last moment. "They're going up as we speak."

I thought he might hyperventilate. Even after I told him it was a joke, it took him nearly a half hour to calm down. Falene nearly choked on her drink recalling the experience.

"There were some good times," I said.

Falene smiled. "There were a lot of good times."

As the evening wore on, our conversation slowed and we began to talk about weightier matters—the final days of our time together.

"I was so worried about you at McKale's funeral," Falene said. "I watched you standing alone next to her casket in the rain." She looked down. "My heart was breaking."

"You were the only one there for me."

She hesitated. "I was really afraid you might take your life."

"Honestly," I said softly, "me too." I reached over and took her hand. "I don't know what I would have done without you."

"I'm glad I could be there for you."

The moment fell into a sweet silence. After a minute I said, "You must be tired."

"I am a little. I didn't sleep well last night."

"I'll let you go. It's been good seeing you."

"You too."

She stood. "I still need to get those tax papers signed. Should we do them tonight or in the morning?"

"The morning's fine," I said. "When are you going back?"

"I was thinking tomorrow afternoon. My brother just got out of rehab and he's living with me."

"Always the good Samaritan," I said.

"Not always," she replied. "Breakfast around ten?"

"Great. Good night, Falene."

"Good night." She leaned forward and kissed me on the cheek, then she turned and walked down the hall. A group of men's heads swiveled as she passed by them. She turned back once more and waved to me.

One of the men said to me in passing, "You are one lucky dude."

I turned away without comment. In the last two months I had lost my wife, my business, my home, and had been beaten and stabbed. And now I'm "lucky." I started laughing on my way to the car.

CHAPTER
Thirty-one

When I am tempted to compare
my life with Job's I remind myself
that he never had a Falene.

Alan Christoffersen's diary

The next morning I picked Falene up at the hotel.
She had already checked out of her room and
was standing with her luggage near the hotel's
front doors. I threw her things in the back seat of
her car, then drove to the IHOP. Our conversation
was light. She told me that a major modeling
agency had discovered her and wanted her to
move to New York.

"You're going to do it, aren't you?" I asked.

She looked vexed. "I don't know. Right now
my brother needs me. We'll see."

After we finished eating I signed the tax
papers, then Falene drove me back to Nicole's
house. We pulled up to the curb, and Falene put
the car in park.

"Thanks for coming," I said. "It's been great
seeing you."

"It's been great seeing you," she replied. "It's
going to be a better year for you."

"That's not setting the bar very high," I said.

"I guess not," she laughed. She brushed her hair back from her face. "Don't forget, you need to decide if I can meet you in Key West."

"I'll let you know."

". . . and you'll call every week."

"Every week. I promise."

She leaned over, and we embraced. "Take care of yourself, Alan."

"You too."

I climbed out of the car and waved again from the sidewalk. She waved back then pulled away from the curb. After she turned the corner I walked back to the apartment. She really was lovely. I wondered when I'd see her again.

CHAPTER
Thirty-two

There is a Chinese curse: May you
live in interesting times. How gladly
I would welcome a boring year.

Alan Christoffersen's diary

New Year's Eve is a drunken night, when police
dispatchers are patching through calls with the
intensity of a fifties telephone operator. Nicole
worked up until 8 P.M., about the time "things
started getting interesting," she said.

Bill was supposed to be over at the house
by eight-thirty, but he never came. This didn't
surprise us, as he called Nicole earlier and said
he felt a little under the weather and might just
sleep it off. "You youngsters are working me
like a rented mule," he said.

Christine was back from Portland, and she
came over around six to help me make cake
doughnuts, one of McKale and my favorite
traditions. We rolled them out, cut them, then
set them in a minifryer to cook. When they were
golden brown we laid them on paper towels
around the kitchen. We made nearly ten dozen,
enough to last for months.

As I think back on that night, I suppose our

party wasn't so much about celebrating a New Year as it was about discarding the old—a year neither Nicole nor I would ever forget as much as we wanted to. A New Year's celebration was the best way I could think of to drive a stake through the last year's heart.

As the clock counted down, we all sat on the couch and watched Dick Clark in Times Square ring in the New Year. At midnight our neighbors emerged from their otherwise docile domains to light firecrackers and bang pans.

"Happy New Year," I said to the women.

"Happy New Year to you too," Nicole said. "And to you, Christine."

"And to both of you," Christine said. "I hope next New Year's finds us all here together just like this."

I glanced over at Nicole. "That would be nice," I said.

Nicole smiled. "That would be nice."

Nicole and I slept in the next morning. It was Saturday and Nicole had the day off. I got up before she did, so I made Belgian waffles with Reddi-wip and sliced strawberries, then called her to breakfast. She came out in her pajamas to eat.

"I really need to keep you around," she said. "I may have to stab you again."

I grimaced. "Now you're scaring me."

When we had finished eating, Nicole said, "We need to take Bill some doughnuts and wish him a happy New Year."

"We have plenty to share," I said. "I'll bag some up."

Bill lived near the hospital in an upscale, older neighborhood called South Hill. His home was a large red brick rambler, surrounded by mature evergreens. His truck was parked in the driveway, and Nicole and I walked together up the stone path to his front porch. Nicole rang his doorbell, but he didn't answer. After a few minutes she knocked on his door, but there was still no response. She turned back to me. "Would you mind checking to see if he's in the garage or backyard?"

"No problem."

I walked around the side of the house, but the garage was locked and his backyard was filled with snow, which had drifted up over his patio. As I was making my way to the back door, I heard Nicole scream. I ran around to the front of the house. The front door was open and inside Nicole was kneeling on the floor next to Bill performing CPR.

"Call 911," she said.

I found the kitchen phone and dialed. "What's the address?" I shouted to Nicole.

"Twenty-two thirteen Yuma."

After I hung up, I walked over and kneeled

197

next to Nicole. I put my hand on Bill's neck to check for a pulse. There was none. His body was cold. I looked up at her. "He's dead, Nicole."

She continued to push on his chest.

"Nicole, he's dead."

"I know," she said. She stopped pushing, covered her eyes, and wept.

CHAPTER
Thirty-three

We can only lose what we
have first claimed.

Alan Christoffersen's diary

Nicole went out and sat in the car and cried, unable to be in the same room as Bill's body. My heart grieved for her more than for Bill. I was certain that Bill was where he wanted to be.

I waited outside for the paramedics and led them inside when they arrived. After examining Bill they made no attempt to revive him.

"When was the last time you saw him alive?" one paramedic asked.

"My friend saw him a couple days ago."

"He's been gone awhile," he said.

Nicole and I spent the rest of the day working through the affairs of Bill's death. The paramedics called the Coroner's Office and they came and took him away. Nicole went through Bill's things looking for someone to call.

While she was looking for contact information, I went downstairs to see the train set she had told me so much about. Bill's train layout was truly remarkable. It was built on heavy boards and elevated, probably 10 by 20 feet, with hundreds of feet of track, tunnels, and miniature towns with plastic buildings.

Bill had left the train's power on, and I pulled on a lever and a small locomotive began winding its way through the Lilliputian landscape. *So that's how the old man spent his time,* I thought.

After some searching, Nicole found a business card for Bill's attorney, Larry Snarr. Fortunately, the card listed a cell phone number, which she immediately dialed and he answered. She told Snarr about Bill's death, and he said he'd take care of everything.

That afternoon Snarr called back for Nicole. "I just heard from the Coroner's Office," he said in a low voice. "Bill died of a massive heart attack shortly after midnight.

"Everything's been set up with the mortuary. He didn't want a funeral service. He told me no one would come, so the mortuary will just bury him."

"That doesn't seem right," Nicole said. "Could we at least have a little graveside service?"

"You just work it out with the mortuary," Snarr said. "He's over at Larkin Mortuary. And let me know if you decide to go ahead with it—I'll be there."

Bill was buried two days later in a plot next to his wife. The mortuary had cleared the snow from the grave, and the casket lay aboveground for our makeshift ceremony. Nicole asked if I would say something, but I declined. McKale's funeral was still too close to me.

There were only four of us that day; Nicole, Christine, Snarr, and me. We gathered in the frozen landscape around the grave, our breath freezing in front of us. Nicole had bought a Christmas wreath, which she laid on top of the casket.

Nicole said, "I just want to say how grateful I am that I got to know Bill. I'm certain that I gained more from our friendship than he did. I'll never forget his love and loyalty for his wife. And I'm glad that he and his sweetheart will be reunited."

Nicole then asked if any of us wanted to say anything. At first I shook my head, but then I said, "I really liked Bill. He had a good heart." Then I felt stupid, thinking, *If he had a* good *heart he'd still be alive.*

Christine said: "Bill was always very good to me. He told me that he was worried that I might slip on the ice, so he put down a little extra rock salt on the walk for me. It may seem like just a small thing, but it made me feel good. I'm glad I got to spend Thanksgiving with him."

Snarr said, "He was an honorable man."

That was it. On the way home Nicole said, "I wonder if I'll have to move."

"Why would you have to move?" I asked.

"New owners."

"I wouldn't start packing," I said. "I'm sure it will take a while before anything happens. Besides, the house has been divided for apartments. Whoever gets it is going to need tenants."

"I hope you're right," she said. "I don't want to move."

Three days later I was doing my aerobics in the living room when someone knocked at the door. It was the attorney, Snarr.

"Is Nicole here?" he asked, standing in the building's lobby.

"She's at work."

"I need to speak with her about Mr. Dodd's estate. Do you know when she'll be home?"

"She's usually home by five-thirty."

"Would it be a problem if I came back tonight for a few minutes?"

"No, that should be fine."

"Very well then. I'll see you this evening."

Nicole arrived home on time. I told her about Larry Snarr's visit as she walked in the door.

"Did he say what he wanted?" she asked.

"He said he needs to talk to you about Bill's estate."

"He's going to kick us out," she said flatly. "Or raise the rent. I don't know where I'm going to find another place at this cost."

"Wait to worry," I said. "Wait to worry."

A couple minutes after six, Snarr pulled up to the house in an older-style Mercedes-Benz. He was wearing a wool overcoat and scarf, and carried a leather briefcase. He walked up the stairway and I met him in the building's lobby. "Come in."

Nicole met him at the apartment door and motioned to the couch. "Have a seat."

"Thank you," he said.

Snarr and I sat on opposite ends of the couch while Nicole sat in an armchair facing us.

"What is this about?" Nicole asked anxiously.

"I am the executor of William Dodd's will."

"Is Nicole in his will?" I asked.

"Actually, Nicole is Mr. Dodd's sole beneficiary." He turned to her. "Bill left everything to you."

"What?" Nicole said.

Snarr opened his briefcase and brought out a dossier. "These documents specifically outline the whole of Mr. Dodd's estate. They include trust funds, life insurance policies, a few mutual funds, and several rental properties, including this property right here. The entire estate is valued at about $3.6 million."

Nicole gasped.

"You're kidding," I said.

"No sir."

"But why me?" Nicole asked.

"Actually, the change was made only two

weeks ago. He did leave a letter for you, perhaps it might explain things." He pulled several documents from the stack he held. "I'll need a few signatures from you, and, as outlined in the will, I'll be deducting my fees from the estate prior to disbursing funds." He handed her several papers. "I've marked where you need to sign."

She signed the documents and handed them back. Snarr put them in his briefcase, then handed her a tan envelope. "Here's the letter Mr. Dodd left for you."

"Thank you," Nicole said.

Snarr stood, lifting his briefcase. "You're very welcome." He handed Nicole a business card. "If you have any questions, please feel free to call at any time."

Nicole walked him to the door. "Thanks for coming by."

"My pleasure," he said.

She shut the door behind him and then turned back and opened the envelope. Inside was a note penned in shaky handwriting.

Dear Angel,

I hope you don't mind me calling you that. It's certainly applicable. If you're reading this, then be happy for me, as I'm finally with my family again.

The last two years have been difficult for me. Ever since I lost my sweetheart,

I lay alone in my cold bed at night listening to the infirmities of my age and hoping for it to catch up to me. The worst infirmity of all has been the loneliness. As you know, June passed several years ago. Our only son, Eric, died nearly twenty years ago. My two brothers and my sister have also died, as have most of my friends. I have no one. Or, I had no one, until this last Thanksgiving when you reached out to me. It may seem a small thing, inviting an old man to join you at the table, but, for me, it was everything. I woke the next day happy for the first time in years. But you didn't end there. You included me in all of your activities. Even with that young man you room with, you brought me along. You made me feel alive again. You were my friend.

I hope you will accept my gift as a token of my friendship. I honestly can't think of anyone more deserving. If you wish, I would hope that you would extend to Christine free rent until she graduates from school. From the bottom of my heart, thank you. You have made an old man smile again.

God bless,
Bill

CHAPTER
Thirty-four

Forgiveness is the key
to the heart's shackles.

Alan Christoffersen's diary

Not surprisingly, Nicole was a little over-whelmed by it all.

"I don't know anything about trusts or real estate. How am I going to handle all this?" she asked. "Will you help me?"

I almost laughed. "That would be the blind leading the blind. But I do know just the man who can."

"Who?"

"My father. The man knows how to handle money."

"That would be perfect," she said.

My father was the only number programmed into the cell phone he gave me, something he'd done himself. I called him and told him about Nicole's windfall. He was pleased and glad to be asked to help.

"I love it when good things happen to good people," he said.

• • •

Nicole went into work the next day and gave her two-weeks' notice. A few days later I accompanied her up to Gonzaga's enrollment office as she enrolled in school and registered for the Spring semester. She was finally going to complete her film studies major with a minor in American literature. She also began writing a new screenplay, one that I think has promise.

"It's the story of a young police dispatcher," she said, "who gets involved in the life of someone she meets through a crime."

I thought she'd probably start looking for a bigger home, but she didn't. "I don't want too many changes in my life right now," Nicole said. "Baby steps."

"Sounds like something my father would say."

"Actually, he did," she replied.

The next three months were filled with so many remarkable changes that the time passed quickly. Nicole was truly a new person, or, more accurately, herself again. She loved going back to school, and she and Christine began carpooling, leaving me with a car during the day, so I got out more and spent several days each week at the Spokane library.

In mid-January, Nicole called her sister, Karen. Karen was relieved to hear from her and apologized for not being there to support her through her accident and Aiden's funeral. "I was just in such a crazy state of mind," Karen said. "But there's no excuse for me not being there for you. I hope you can someday forgive me."

"I forgive you now," Nicole said.

Those four words had a miraculous effect on both women. They made plans to get together that summer and vacation at Bullman Beach for old times' sake.

While I waited for better weather, I stepped up my physical training. I walked twice a day or swam at the community center when the weather was inclement.

I had gone through my road atlas so many times I could recite the towns and cities I would pass through on my way to South Dakota.

My muscle mass had returned and the pain I had overcome was just a bad memory. I was getting antsy to leave, and it seemed that with each new day I felt more acutely my own path calling me.

Spokane had a mild winter that year, and around March the snow on the ground had completely melted. Every day I'd watch the weather reports, and Nicole had taken it upon herself to call Yellowstone National Park daily to check on road conditions.

Saturday afternoon, March 19, I had just finished my morning walk when I found Nicole sitting on the outside steps of her building waiting for my return.

"How was your walk?" she asked. She looked upset.

"What's wrong?" I asked.

"I don't want to tell you."

"Tell me what?"

"If I answer that, then I've told you, which is precisely what I don't want to do." She stood up and walked inside. I followed her in.

When I had closed the apartment door, Nicole said, "The east gate of Yellowstone is open."

"Oh," I said.

We were both quiet for a moment.

"When will you leave?" she asked.

"I'll need a couple days."

She looked down. "Then we have a couple days. How do you want to spend them?"

"I've got some preparations I need to make."

"Anything else?"

"What do you want to do?"

"I don't care. Just as long as I'm with you."

CHAPTER
Thirty-five

I don't think it is as much a
human foible as it is a human curse
that we cannot understand the beauty
of a thing until it is gone.

Alan Christoffersen's diary

I woke Tuesday to the smell of bacon and coffee. I pulled on my sweat pants and walked out of my room. Nicole was in the kitchen. She had made me breakfast. "Morning, deserter."

"Good morning."

"Would you like some coffee, Mr. Abandonment?"

I grinned. "Is this necessary?"

"I think so, Mr. Exit. How about you stay until tomorrow."

"You'll say the same thing tomorrow."

"It's the magic of tomorrow. It never comes."

I sat down and she sat across from me. "How far are you planning on walking today?" she asked.

"I wanted to make it to Coeur d'Alene, but I'll probably end up just over the border into Idaho."

She lifted a piece of bacon and took a bite. "What an adventure."

As I looked at her, I realized that we'd been together for almost five months. It was hard to believe that she wouldn't be there every day. The thought made my heart ache. Difficult times build unique relationships, and we'd become closer than friends. She was the sister I'd never had.

Her eyes began to well with tears. "You have no idea how much I'm going to miss you," she said softly.

After breakfast I showered and shaved, fully appreciating the hot water I'd soon be deprived of, then I went into my room and checked the contents of my pack one more time. When I was ready, I put on my Akubra hat and carried my pack out to the front room. "It's time," I said.

Nicole walked out of her bedroom. Her eyes were red and puffy. She took my hand and we walked out together, stopping at the house's front door. "I better not go outside," she said, "or I'll probably just keep on following you."

I leaned my pack against the wall and took her hands in mine. There was a sweet awkwardness to the moment, like icing on sorrow. I looked into her eyes. "So, did you ever figure out why you came to help me?"

"Maybe I'm just the kind of girl who rescues stray puppies."

I squeezed her hands.

Nicole said, "I've realized that the happiest

times of my life have been when I was taking care of someone—my Aiden, you, then Bill. I'm going to miss having someone to care for."

"I have a feeling that won't last long."

"Why do you say that?"

"The world is full of stray puppies."

She smiled sadly. "Do you have your St. Christopher?"

"Yes," I said, pulling the chain out of my shirt.

For a moment we just gazed into each other's eyes then she suddenly threw her arms around me, burying her head in my chest. She began to cry again. "Will you call me when you get to Key West?"

"Absolutely."

She looked up into my eyes. "Please don't forget me."

I wiped a tear from her cheek. "How would I do that?"

"Will you be mad at me if I call you sometime? I promise I won't stalk you."

"You call if you ever need anything. And remember to let my dad help you."

She kept looking at me, as tears ran down her face.

I kissed her forehead, then she buried her head in my chest again. "What would I have done without you?"

I just silently held her. It's not that there wasn't anything to say. It's that there was too much and words were poor substitutes for our feelings. It was maybe ten minutes before she sighed and stepped back. "I'll let you go," she said softly.

I grabbed my backpack, lifting it over my shoulder. Nicole stood with her arms folded, occasionally wiping a tear from her cheek.

I took a deep breath. "See you," I said.

"See you," she echoed.

I walked outside and I was alone again.

CHAPTER
Thirty-six

Last night the reality of my impending departure hit me. My former companions—Loneliness and Despair—had been patiently waiting outside Nicole's house the whole time, waiting to get me alone, waiting to resume our walk.

—Alan Christoffersen's diary

In the storm of the emotional challenges of my departure, I had neglected to consider the physical ones. I was leaving the creature comforts of Nicole's home for the exposure, tedium, and exertion of the rugged outdoors. Even if the roads were open, it was still very cold.

In the east I could see dark storm clouds gathering like an angry mob. The clouds reminded me of the night I had spent in the shacks outside Leavenworth, being pelted by hail.

I walked east on Nora to Dakota Street, then south, past the Montessori. At Mission, I turned left and walked east again for several miles until I came to Greene, turned south and walked another quarter mile to Trent, the road that would take me to the Washington-Idaho border.

The scenery on Trent changed dramatically for the worse as suburb turned to industrial—I passed steel and aluminum buildings, a junkyard, a boiler company, equipment rental, auto repair shops, and Bobo's Adult Video.

Still, the names of the coffee purveyors were no less creative than what I'd passed between Seattle and Spokane—the Grind Finale, Grind Central Station, Caffiends Espresso, Sorrentino's Espresso, and 1st Shot Gourmet Espresso.

About four hours into my walk I stopped to get a coffee at the Java the Hut, then sat behind the small wooden shack and ate lunch from my pack. As I sat there sipping from my cup, I spotted a big reflective sign that read:

Apple Maggot Quarantine Area

The sign raised many questions: Were people actually carrying apple maggots, and would the sign stop them if they were? Were there areas where apple maggots were considered okay? Would other types of maggots be welcome? Would apple maggots someday be an endangered species and have SAVE THE APPLE MAGGOTS bumper stickers?

I rested for about a half hour, then set off

again. Later that afternoon nature returned and the landscape grew dense and green again until it opened up into a broad, welcome expanse of horse property.

Standing next to the road was a cinnamon-colored quarter horse that looked remarkably like McKale's. The horse watched me approach, her head hovering over the vinyl fence. I stopped and rubbed her nose, then I took an apple from my pack and gave it to her.

An hour later I reached the Idaho state line. Emotionally, this had a remarkable effect on me. After six months I was finally out of Washington. This small step seemed to legitimize my journey and raise my hopes that I might someday actually reach my destination.

A few miles later, in the town of Post Falls, I stopped at a gas station for an energy drink and to ask about distances and lodging. The lady behind the counter informed me that I had *only* another 10 miles to Coeur d'Alene. "Just a few minutes ahead," she said, apparently not noticing my backpack.

"Is there anything closer?" I asked.

"There's a Comfort Inn just down the road, but if I were you, I'd just go on to Coeur d'Alene. Great lodging there, and it's a beautiful town."

I thanked her, paid for my drink, then walked back out to the street. I spotted the Comfort Inn a few blocks down on the north side of the highway. I downed my energy drink, then headed toward the hotel.

The Comfort Inn was small, tidy, and just $75 a night, which included a continental breakfast. I paid with my credit card and went to my room on the second floor. I lay my pack on the floor near the closet, then reclined back on the bed to rest a moment before going back out to find dinner. I woke the next morning.

CHAPTER
Thirty-seven
Today God dropped someone else in my path.

Alan Christoffersen's diary

I woke confused. The sun shone brightly through the window, and I rolled over and looked at the digital clock. It was already 9:09. It took me a moment to realize the time was A.M., not P.M. I was still fully dressed, boots and all, and lying on top of the covers. My legs were sore and I sat up and rubbed my calves.

I showered, dressed, and then went downstairs with my pack. I grabbed an apple and a cheese Danish from the hotel's complimentary selection, then checked out, stopping for a coffee at the aptly named Jumpstart Java. I arrived in Coeur d'Alene just before noon.

I knew three things about Coeur d'Alene. First, they had a world-class Christmas celebration. Nicole and I had agreed that our visit to see the lights was well worth the trip.

Second, the scenery was remarkably beautiful. Travel brochures to the city touted that no less than Barbara Walters had called Coeur d'Alene "a little slice of heaven" and put it on her list of "most fascinating places to visit."

The third thing I knew about Coeur d'Alene seemed wildly in contrast to the first two—that it was the headquarters of the Aryan Nations white supremacy group. In 1998, Coeur d'Alene made national news when there had been a standoff between federal agents and the group, ending with some of the group's leaders being arrested.

That Coeur d'Alene is a town of contrast is evident even in its name. The name sounds romantic (*The Heart of Alene*), but it's not. "Alene" isn't a person and the name was meant as a slur. French fur traders named the indigenous tribe the Coeur d'Alene—Heart of the Awl —meaning that they were sharp-hearted, or shrewd.

The resort town's hired spin doctors have either ignored this fact or tried to pass off the insult as a term of endearment, but native French speakers visiting the city agree that it was not meant kindly.

Once inside the city, I stopped at a small market and bought bottled water, deli rolls, trail mix, a few apples and oranges, chocolate bars, pecorino cheese, a box of energy bars, a carton of Egg Beaters (which I packed in a plastic bag full of ice), and some dry salami. With my pack substantially heavier, I walked up Sherman Avenue, perusing the quaint shops and boutiques that lined the downtown district.

Coeur d'Alene is the kind of town that McKale would have loved. She would have spent the day gleaning obscure facts about the city and its residents, returning to our hotel room at night with her arms needled through the handles of shopping bags and regurgitating everything she'd learned. I was disappointed that I had never brought her.

The people of Coeur d'Alene (CDA, they call it) are as verbose as they are friendly—which is a polite way of saying they like to talk. A lot. I found myself trapped in several stores. I have nothing against friendly; I just didn't have the time for it.

I walked through the city center and climbed the on-ramp to I-90, a fairly busy highway, but the only route I could find to cross the mountains. The highway was busier than Washington's Highway 2, and the cars drove faster. On the plus side, the highway had a wider shoulder. A mile up I passed a road sign for the next town:

Kellogg, Idaho
36 miles

The town was too far to make, which meant I'd have to camp along the way.

Around noon I crossed the Centennial Bridge, with its breathtaking view of Lake Coeur d'Alene. Shortly after the bridge, the road began to descend steeply while the lake continued on to the south, specked with houseboats and lake homes.

There was really no place to get off the highway, so I didn't stop for lunch but ate an energy bar and an orange and kept walking. About 10 miles and two and a half hours later, the lake gave way to grazing land and cow-inhabited meadows. A sign proclaimed the gateway to the Idaho Panhandle National Forest.

The sun was starting to set behind me when I reached the Fourth of July Pass recreation area, and I was tired and ready to find a place to camp and eat dinner. I took the off ramp, which ended in a T, unsure of which way to go. The top sign pointed right to a recreation area for motorized vehicles, located somewhere out of sight up a long steep hill. The sign below read MULLAN TREE, with an arrow pointing left to a declining asphalt road, which, on weary legs, looked infinitely more inviting. I chose left.

I had no idea that the simple decision I had just made would affect so many lives.

I crossed back over the interstate and climbed a slight incline up to a gravel road. A brown Forest Service sign explained that the Mullan Tree was a lodgepole pine that was carved more than 150 years ago by some of General John Mullan's soldiers to commemorate the completion of the Mullan Military Road, the first major highway in the Pacific Northwest, which ran between Fort Benton, Montana, and Fort Walla Walla, Washington. (The Mullan name would become familiar to me, for I soon learned that Mullan had a propensity for naming everything after himself.)

The road split again and a sign informed me that the celebrated tree was located on the left fork up the mountain. Unfortunately, the sign gave no clue as to just how far up the road the tree was. Looking up the steep grade, I decided that I hadn't the legs, curiosity, or daylight to explore, so I took the right trail, which ended about 50 yards from the fork at a small recreational area with a large stone statue honoring General Mullan. I set to making camp.

I walked off the gravel-dirt road, down a slope to a small, flat area with an outhouse and a couple of picnic tables. The air was cool and thick with a mossy aroma. The NO OVERNIGHT CAMPING signs posted all around didn't worry me. I doubted anyone ever checked on this obscure little stop, and even if they did, it would be easy enough to hide my tent in the thick vegetation.

I hiked back near the picnic tables and constructed my tent behind a grove of trees where it couldn't be seen from the road even in broad daylight.

I was famished. The deli rolls I bought in Coeur d'Alene were smashed to half their thickness, but they still tasted all right. I cut thick pieces of salami and pecorino, and spread the smashed bread with mayonnaise and mustard from the little condiment packets I'd picked up at one of the fast-food joints along the way. I devoured the sandwich quickly so I made myself another, which I ate with a Hershey's almond bar.

I had finished the second sandwich and climbed into my tent when I heard the spit of gravel from an approaching vehicle as it drove past my camp and skidded to an abrupt stop. I heard the doors open, releasing a party of voices, mostly bass in tone, with the occasional higher-pitched voice of a young woman. The vehicle's inhabitants were laughing and talking excitedly, and I guessed it was probably a group of drunk college kids.

The area was mostly in shadows by that time and I was invisible behind a darkened screen of forest. I was sure that I had no reason to worry, but after my mugging, I was still on edge. I reached into my pack and brought out my father's gun. I pulled out the clip I kept in a separate part of my pack and locked it into place. Just in case.

Then I heard the woman scream. "Just leave me alone!"

Her scream was followed by the slamming of doors and more dull laughter.

"Stop it!" she shouted.

I couldn't hear what the men were saying, but their voices were low and taunting. I checked my gun's safety, then slid it down my waistband and crawled out of my tent. I quietly crept up the rise, peering from behind a tree to see what was happening.

A 4-door Dodge pickup was parked near the monument, its headlamps illuminating the statue. To the rear right of the truck were four young men and an even younger woman. All the men, except for one, had surrounded her, and she was swinging at them.

The young man who was standing apart from the others, a lanky, blond kid, seemed to be nervously advocating for the girl. The ringleader of the bunch was a muscular kid, probably in his early twenties, and built like a football lineman. In one hand he held a can of beer. He turned back and told the blond kid to "Shut the hell up." Even in the dim light I could see the cruelty on the man's face.

Then the girl spit at him, and he backhanded her across her jaw, knocking her to the ground. She held her cheek and cried, "Please, stop."

"We gave you a ride, you're gonna pay for it," he said. He threw his half-full beer can at her, which splashed up on the ground in front of her.

"I don't owe you anything," she said. "Just let me go."

He walked up to her side. "Not until you make good. Take your clothes off."

"No."

"Fine, we'll take them off."

She snarled, "Are you a rapist? That's a class-one felony." She turned to the other guys, "Are you rapists too?"

I was impressed by her courage. All the men seemed taken back by her reasoning except the ringleader. "Shut up! Just take 'em off."

"You'll have to do it."

"You heard her, dudes, she asked me to."

He moved toward her and she, still sitting in the dirt and gravel, began to scuttle back. He ran behind her and grabbed her hair while she futilely swung at him, her blows only serving to make him angrier. He yelled out a guttural string of profanities, then grabbed her T-shirt and yanked on it, ripping it across the shoulder.

I had seen enough. I climbed out to the edge of the gravel road and shouted, "Leave her alone."

Everything froze. The men were clearly surprised to discover they weren't alone and everyone turned to me, including the girl. For a moment no one moved or said anything.

I took a few steps closer. "Get away from her. Now."

The ringleader scowled at me. "This isn't your business. Walk away, or we'll make it your business."

My eyes panned across the four of them as I continued to walk forward. "I said get away from her."

Ringleader looked at me with a dumbfounded expression. "Are you stupid? Four of us, one of you. You're outnumbered, loser."

I stopped about 20 feet from them. I grasped the handle of my gun and pulled it out. I held it up as I clicked off the safety. "I've got the math right. Four of you, sixteen rounds in the clip. I've got *you* four to one."

The gun had their full attention. I pointed the barrel at the blond kid's stomach. "This is how it's going down. You walk away from her right now, or I'm going to shoot the tall glass of water first, then Big Ears, Fat Boy, and I save you for last." I squared off at the blond kid, holding both hands on the gun. "You've got five seconds to walk away."

Trembling, the kid raised his hands, even though I hadn't told him to. "I wasn't doing anything. Tim, get away from her. Let's go."

"He's bluffing," Ringleader said.

"You think I'm bluffing?" I asked. "Five months ago I got stabbed by some losers like you. That's when I got the gun. I will definitely kill all of you and not lose a bit of sleep. Enough talking, I'm counting to five then I'm going to start firing. Ready, Slim? One . . ."

The blond was shaking with fear. "We're leaving, man. We're going. C'mon, Tim," he screamed. "Get away from her!"

". . . two . . . three."

Ringleader kicked at the girl, sneered, then turned. "We're leaving," he said to the two men next to him (who looked visibly relieved). "C'mon."

"I need my backpack," the girl said.

"Where is it?" I asked.

"It's in the back of the truck," she said.

The lanky kid reached over the side of the truck's bed and pulled out a medium-sized backpack. He set it on the ground with surprising gentility. "Here you go."

Ringleader started around the truck, saying things beneath his breath. I pointed the gun at him. "Stop."

He froze.

"If you get the idea to drive your truck at me, or her, I won't stop shooting until you're all dead. If you lose your mind and come back later, I'll be waiting in the dark for you, just like we did in Desert Storm. No warning. Trust me, I'll know. This gravel pops like firecrackers— I heard you coming before you left the off-ramp."

The second kid, the one I'd called "Big Ears,"

spoke for the first time. "No worries, man. We're out of here."

I kept the gun leveled at them as they climbed in their truck. Ringleader revved the engine a couple times, then put the truck in gear. The wheels spun out and the truck fishtailed, but they kept a good distance from me. They drove up to the fork, then, shouting out obscenities, drove off.

When we were alone, I pushed the safety on the gun and slid it back in my waistband. I turned to the girl. "Are you okay?"

"Yeah," she said, climbing to her feet.

"You were brave," I said.

"So were you."

"No, I just had a gun." I walked toward her. "How did you end up with them?"

"I was hitchhiking and they picked me up."

"Not a good idea."

"I didn't know they were creeps." She wasn't quite as shaken as I expected her to be. "Were you really in the army?"

"No," I said. "Advertising."

She smirked. "Is that even a real gun?"

"Yes."

She brushed off the back of her pants, then walked over and lifted her pack. As she neared, she looked younger to me than I had originally thought. I guessed her to be seventeen.

"Do you have anything to eat?" she asked.

"I can make you a sandwich. I've got cheese and salami."

"I'll eat anything."

"Come with me."

She followed me back toward my tent.

"What's your name?" she asked.

I reached into the tent and brought out my pack. "Alan. Yours?"

She sat down at the picnic table, laying her own pack across it. "Kailamai."

"Kay—la—may?" I repeated, distinctly pronouncing each syllable.

She nodded. "Yeah."

"Sounds Hawaiian."

"Samoan."

"You don't look Samoan."

"I know."

I took out the bread, meat, and cheese. "The bread's kind of smashed."

"I'm not fussy."

I pulled out my knife and cut off a slice of cheese, then salami. "Mayo?"

She nodded. "Yes, please."

I cut the roll in half, then took out one of the packets of mayonnaise and spread it across the bread with the packet. I put the bread and cheese inside then handed her the sandwich.

"Thank you," she said. She ravenously bit into it. I wondered when she had last eaten.

"Hungry?" I asked facetiously.

She answered my question with another bite. Then she said with a full mouth, "I haven't eaten since yesterday."

"There's more, if you want."

"Thank you." She continued to chew. After a few more bites she slowed down. "Did you really get stabbed?"

"Three times. I was walking along the highway outside Spokane when a gang jumped me."

"You walk a lot?"

"You could say that."

"Where are you headed?"

"Key West."

"Where's that?"

"In Florida."

She looked at me as if she were trying to tell if I was joking. "You've got a lot of walking to do."

I sat down at the end of the picnic bench. "Where are you headed?"

"Back east to live with my aunt."

"Where back east?"

"Boston."

"That's a long way to hitchhike."

She shrugged. "I don't have a car."

"You could have flown. Or taken a bus."

"I could have if I had any money."

"How old are you?"

My question seemed to trouble her. She

stopped eating, then slowly looked up. "You're not going to do anything to me, are you?"

"Didn't I just stop those guys from hurting you?"

"Well, maybe you just wanted me for yourself."

"I'm not that kind of guy."

"I thought all guys were that kind of guy."

"Not by a long shot," I said.

After a moment, she said, "I'm almost eighteen."

"Where are your parents?"

"My mom's dead. I don't know where my father is." She said this casually as she took another bite of sandwich.

"Sorry," I said.

When she finished chewing, she asked, "About what?"

"Huh?"

"What are you sorry about?" she asked. "That my mom's dead or that I don't know where my father is?"

"Both."

"I don't care about my father. I don't even know who he is. He could be you for all I know. At least if you were older. And I'm not sorry my mother's dead. No one is."

I just looked at her for a moment. "Then I'm sorry for that too." I breathed out and I could now see my breath in the chill air. Neither of us spoke for a few minutes as she ate. "How's your sandwich?" I asked.

"Good, thank you."

"I have a Hershey's chocolate bar if you want it."

"That sounds really good."

I retrieved the candy from my pack and brought it over to her. "Here you go. If you want to camp with me tonight, you can sleep in the tent."

"Thank you," she said, taking the candy. She peeled the bar like a banana. She took a small bite, then looked up at me. "So what are you running away from?"

"What makes you think I'm running away from something?"

"You're a nice guy, you talk like you're smart, and you're good-looking, so there's no way you don't have something you're leaving, like a girlfriend and a job. So you must be running away from something."

I was impressed by her reasoning. "I *was* married."

"Oh," she said, nodding as if she understood. "Bad divorce."

"No divorce. She died."

She looked genuinely upset by this. "I'm sorry. What did she die of?"

"She was in an accident. Her horse got spooked and threw her."

"I'm sorry," she said again.

"So am I. She was everything to me. I lived for her."

She was silent for a moment, then said, "That must be nice though, having someone to live for."

"It's nice until you lose them." I handed her a bottle of water. She took a long draw and handed it back. "I think I'll go to bed," I said. "Like I said, you can sleep in the tent."

"Where are you going to sleep?"

"Under the stars."

"It's cold out here."

"I'll be all right."

She looked back over at the tent. "I don't care if we share the tent. I trust you. Besides, it will be cozy."

There were at least a dozen reasons not to share the tent, but the chill in the air was pretty persuasive. "All right."

"Do you have enough for another sandwich?"

"Sure."

I made her a second sandwich, then went inside the tent, undressed, and climbed into my sleeping bag. Maybe five minutes later she said, "Knock, knock."

"You can come in," I said.

She threw her sleeping bag inside, then crawled in after it. She climbed into her bag with her clothes still on. After a minute she said, "This is kind of nice."

"The tent?"

"Yes." More silence. "Do you mind if I pray?"

"No."

"I usually pray out loud," she said. "Do you mind?"

"No."

She rolled over on her stomach and covered her face with her hands. "Dear Father in heaven, thank you for another day. Thank you for all that you've given me. Thank you for sending an angel my way tonight. I am grateful for Alan and his protection and the food and shelter he's given me. Please bless him with peace and safety and all that he needs. And I pray for those who are being hurt tonight and please send angels to save them too. I pray that those guys in the truck won't come back. In the name of Jesus, Amen."

We were both quiet for a moment. She rolled back over. "Do you think those guys will come back?"

"No."

"I don't know," she said. "They were pretty crazy."

"I hate to think what would have happened if I hadn't been here," I said.

"Same thing as usual," she replied, and rolled away from me. "Good night."

It was the last thing she said before she fell asleep.

CHAPTER
Thirty-eight

I wonder what McKale would say
if she saw me now. Actually I know.
She'd call me a "crazy old coot!"
Either that or smack me.

Alan Christoffersen's diary

I woke the next morning at sunrise. The inside of the tent was warm, and drops of water had condensed on the inclined vinyl ceiling. It took me a moment to remember why I wasn't alone and who was sleeping next to me.

Kailamai was still asleep, on her side, lightly snoring. I dressed inside my sleeping bag then climbed out of the tent.

The morning air was chill and crisp, and the sun was just breaking through the thick canopy of forest, which was filled with the shrill single-note calls of an owl, invisible in the trees above me.

I had not fallen right to sleep. Instead, I had thought about the last thing Kailamai had said. "Same as usual." I wondered about her story—her father (or lack of one) and a dead mother she claimed no one cared about, including her.

I gathered some cantaloupe-sized stones and

made a fire pit, then walked around the area picking up branches until I had collected an armful. I could have used my propane stove to cook breakfast, but it was a cold morning and I wanted the warmth of the fire and thought the girl probably would as well.

I put three of the stones in the center of the pit, and when the flames were a foot high, I balanced my pan on the stones. A minute later I poured in the carton of Egg Beaters. I cut thin slices of pecorino and salami and dropped them across the bubbling egg.

Kailamai emerged from the tent about five minutes later. "Hey," she said. I turned around. I had only seen her in the dark, so I was now seeing her clearly for the first time. She was about five foot three, thin, with a wide face. She was prettier than I had realized, in a classical way, with high cheekbones and a gentle, sloping nose like one of the women in a Botticelli painting. Her hair was dark and tousled. She also had piercings I hadn't noticed, three in each ear and one in her nose.

"Whatever you're making smells good," she said.

"A different rendition of what you ate last night. Omelets with pecorino and salami."

"Sounds good," she said. She straddled the picnic table's bench, close enough to the fire to feel its heat.

"Hungry?" I asked.

"I was born hungry."

"Grab that mess kit," I said.

"The what?"

"The mess kit. It's that silver thing on top of my pack."

She lifted the kit. "This?"

"Yeah. Just bring it over."

"Why do you call it a mess kit?"

"I don't know. It's an army thing."

"I thought you said you weren't in the army."

"I wasn't," I said. I took the kit apart and spooned an omelet into one of the halves. "Here you go."

She took the food, then sat down at the table, her back to the fire. "Thanks. I'll say grace."

I took the pan from the fire. "All right."

"Heavenly Father, thank you for this food, and bless Alan for sharing it with me. Bless this food to our bodies' health and us to Thy service, Amen."

"Amen," I said. I flopped the remaining omelet into my metal bowl, then sat down next to her. "You pray a lot," I said.

"Before meals. When I get up. When I go to bed. Whenever I'm afraid. Whenever I feel grateful." She smiled at me. "Pretty much all the time." She took a bite of omelet. "It's good to have a hot breakfast."

"I wish I had some coffee to go with it," I

said. I took a large bite of omelet. "What are your plans today? More hitchhiking?"

"I guess." She looked down for a moment, picking at her food. "If you don't mind, I'd like to walk with you for a while."

I wasn't sure if this was a good idea or not. "I walk more than twenty miles a day. Think you can keep up?"

"I'll try."

I took a bite and slowly chewed while I considered her request.

"If you don't want me to walk with you, I understand," she said.

"It's okay," I decided. "I wouldn't mind some company."

She smiled. "Good. Me too."

After she'd finished eating, she stood holding her plate. "I'm going to see if I can find some water to wash our dishes." She came back a few minutes later with a clean, dripping pan. "I found a water spigot."

"Do you think it's potable?" I asked.

"What's potable?"

"Is it safe to drink?"

"I don't know. It didn't say it wasn't."

"Then it probably is. We better fill up." I took a long drink from my canteen and then got two plastic bottles. "Where is it?"

"It's over there," she said, pointing. "Behind the statue."

I filled my receptacles then came back and poured out one of the bottles on the fire, the ash and rock releasing a white cloud of smoke and steam. I went and filled it again and stowed it in my pack.

We rolled up our sleeping bags and Kailamai helped me break down the tent. I put on my hat and sunglasses. When all was packed, I asked, "Ready?"

She slid her own pack over her shoulders. "I'm ready."

We climbed the hill to the road and up to the fork. As we passed the Forest Service sign, I asked, "Have you ever seen the Mullan Tree?"

"Never heard of it. Is it worth seeing?"

I looked up the road where the sign pointed, then just kept walking. "Apparently not," I said.

We crossed the interstate, then walked down the on-ramp to I-90. The road was still descending, and I pulled down the rim of my Akubra hat as the sun was in my eyes.

"I like your hat," Kailamai said.

"It's an Akubra," I said. "I got it in Australia."

"You've been to Australia?"

"About five years ago. I had a client from Melbourne."

"That's cool. I've always wanted to go there."

"I hear Boston's nice," I said. "You have an aunt there?"

"I just made that up," she said. "It was just the first place that came to mind."

"Where are you really going?"

"I don't know. I thought that if I walked long enough I'd find something."

"Where's your home?"

"I don't have one. Technically, I'm a runaway. At least on the state's records. But only for another month."

"What do you mean by that?"

"I'm a foster kid. I've been in the system for most of my life. My last foster home didn't really work out, so I ran away."

"Why didn't you just go back to the state?"

"There's no point. I'm eighteen in a month, so the state's no longer responsible for me. It's called aging out. I'm on my own."

"Are you ready to be on your own?"

"I guess I'll find out. The odds aren't good. My caseworker told me that two years after aging out, there's a sixty percent chance I'll be pregnant, in jail, homeless, or dead. But I'm not going to let that happen. I want to make something of my life. I want to go to college."

"Do you know what you want to study?"

"I want to be a judge someday."

I nodded. "That's a great goal. Everyone would have to call you 'Your Honor.'"

A broad smile crossed her lips. "That would be awesome. Maybe I could be like Judge Judy

240

and have my own TV show. Judge Judy doesn't take anyone's junk."

"No," I said. "She doesn't."

I liked this girl.

CHAPTER
Thirty-nine

This is the joke Kailamai told me today.
A wife asked her husband,
"How was the golfing today?"
"It was awful," he replied. "On the eleventh
hole Harry had a heart attack and died."
"Oh no!" she exclaimed. "That is awful!"
"You're telling me," the husband replied.
"For the next seven holes it was hit the ball,
drag Harry. Hit the ball, drag Harry."

Alan Christoffersen's diary

We had walked about two and a half miles when
we came to the Old Mission State Park. The Old
Mission of the Sacred Heart was built by Jesuit
priests in 1853 and is the oldest building standing in Idaho. Even by today's standards it's an
impressive structure, and it's hard to believe
these men built this massive edifice in such a
secluded place without the benefit of a lumber-
yard or heavy machinery. What they lacked in
technology they made up for in devotion.

The park was open to visitors and Kailamai
and I spent an hour wandering around the visitors'
center. That morning I discovered two things

about Kailamai. First, that she was funny.

"How many psychiatrists does it take to change a lightbulb?" she asked.

"No idea," I said.

"Just one. But the lightbulb has to *want* to change."

I grinned. "That's pretty funny."

She continued. "These guys rob a bank wearing gorilla masks. As they're getting away, a customer pulls off one of the men's masks to see what he looks like. The bank robber says, 'Now that you've seen me, you have to die,' and he shoots the man dead. The robber looks around the room. Everyone is looking away or covering their eyes. 'Did anyone else see my face?' he asks. An Irishman in the corner slowly raised his hand. 'You saw my face?' the bank robber asked. 'No, but I think my wife might have got a wee peek.' "

I laughed pretty hard.

The second thing I discovered about Kailamai is that she could outeat me. I made salami sandwiches again and gave her an apple and a couple energy bars. She devoured it all. We walked all day and reached the Kellogg city limits as the sun began to set. Kailamai was exhausted and I slowed my pace considerably so she could keep up. She never complained about the distance, but several times apologized for slowing me down and said if I needed to leave her I could. I didn't want to. I liked her company. In some ways she reminded me of McKale when she was younger: bright, funny, and sardonic.

Kellogg is a peculiar town, divided by the interstate between old and new—the new being a ski resort with one of the largest gondolas in the western hemisphere.

According to town lore, Kellogg has the proud distinction of being founded by a jackass. Literally. The town is named after a prospector named Noah Kellogg. One morning in 1885, Kellogg's donkey wandered off from his camp. Several hours later Kellogg found the animal standing next to a large outcropping of galena, a lead ore mineral that contains significant deposits of silver.

The discovery led to the establishment of the Bunker Hill Mine and Smelter, which was operational for more than a hundred years, until closing in 1981. A sign outside the city read:

This is the town founded by a jackass and inhabited by his descendants

Kailamai assured me that this was true. "I know," she said. "I used to live here."

We crossed the interstate to the old part of town and went inside the Silverhorn Motor Inn and the Silver Spoon Restaurant. The front lobby was small and cluttered with various sundries for sale or borrow: bottles of toothpaste, toothbrushes, shampoo, and shaving cream, and an entire wall of ancient VHS videotapes.

I asked for two rooms but Kailamai objected. "That's too much money. Let's just get one room with two beds."

"It doesn't seem proper," I said.

"You were like two inches from me in the tent," she replied.

She had a point. I asked for one room.

The woman handed me a key to room 255 and informed us that the hotel had VCRs in each room and the videos were all free to borrow. She also warned us to be careful on the roads, as one of the restaurant's waitresses had been hit by a bear while driving the night before.

"He just ran right into the side of her car. Poor girl was shaking like a leaf."

I sent Kailamai to the restaurant while I carried both of our packs to the room, then came down and joined her.

"I don't have much money," Kailamai told me as she looked over the menu. She had already eaten a dinner roll and was buttering a second.

"Don't worry, it's my treat."

She looked relieved. "Thanks."

"You're welcome."

I ordered for us two "Nancy Melts"—a house

specialty burger on grilled sourdough with bacon, grilled onions, Swiss cheese, and sautéed mushrooms, and for dessert we had huckleberry pie à la mode.

That night as we lay in our beds, Kailamai asked, "How far do you think we walked today?"

"About twenty-six miles," I said.

"I've never walked that far before." She was quiet a moment. "How far are we walking tomorrow?"

"About the same," I said.

"Okay," she said. "Night."

"You did great today, Kailamai. I'm proud of you."

"Thanks." She knelt by the side of her bed and said her prayers.

CHAPTER
Forty

We reached Montana today. Along
the way we met the most interesting
of characters—Pete the miner.
The heavens indeed hold many
stars from which to set a course.

Alan Christoffersen's diary

The next morning we had breakfast at the hotel's restaurant—pancakes and bacon with scrambled eggs. We left the hotel and then stopped next door at a convenience store for bottled water, trail mix, and beef jerky. We didn't worry about dinner. There were towns close enough that we'd be eating at a restaurant that night.

We crossed the interstate bridge and continued our walk. After a few miles Kailamai said, "This might seem like a dumb question, but do you know how to get to Key West?"

I hid my smile. "Basically. I've got maps."

"Shouldn't we be walking more south?"

"After Butte, Montana, I'm planning to walk southeast through Yellowstone."

"We're walking through Yellowstone?"

I was curious that she'd included herself on my journey. "I was planning on it."

"I've heard that there are a lot of buffalo there. I've always wanted to see a buffalo in real life."

"That would be cool," I said.

Maybe an hour later she asked, "Do you believe in UFOs and aliens, that kind of stuff?"

"No. But I know where there's a crop circle," I said. "Wilbur, Washington. I walked past it."

"I think I've figured out where aliens come from."

"Where?" I asked, genuinely wanting to hear her theory.

"From Earth."

"Explain," I said.

"My theory is that aliens aren't in flying saucers, they're in time machines."

"What do you mean?"

"Think about it. If time travel is possible . . ."

"A big *if*," I said.

"Yeah, but people used to say that about flying. Now everyone is doing it. So let's say that there are things we don't understand yet about time, which is logical, or at least possible, right?"

"I'll give you that."

"So if it is possible to move through time, that means that there are people already here, observing us."

"Why would they want to do that?"

"Same reason we study history. Besides, wouldn't you want to see the past if you could?

Watch Lincoln give the Gettysburg Address, or listen to the Sermon on the Mount?"

"But then we'd see them around us. The physicist Stephen Hawking said, 'The absence of tourists from the future is an argument against the existence of time travel.' "

"Haven't you ever read a book about time travel?" Kailamai said. "People from the future can't show themselves or be involved in our circumstances or they could mess things up and change history."

"History is messed up."

"Yeah, but if they did, they might disappear. You know, like in all the science fiction movies."

"So you think aliens are us?"

"It makes sense, doesn't it? The way people describe aliens, with two eyes, our body shape, smaller bodies. As technology takes over, it makes sense that our brains would evolve bigger and our bodies grow smaller."

"You're a very interesting young woman," I said.

"Thanks," she said.

Near the Kellogg city limit, Kailamai pointed to a car dealership north of the freeway. "That's Dave Smith Motors. It's one of the biggest car dealerships in the world."

I thought it odd to find such a large dealership so far from a metropolitan area.

"I used to go to school there, right by the used car lot. Dave Smith tore down my elementary school to build his dealership. We were the Sunshine Unicorns."

"The Sunshine Unicorns?"

"I know, pretty lame, huh? Probably a good thing he tore it down."

Four and a half miles down the road we saw signs for something called the Sunshine Miners Memorial, which struck me as a peculiarly cheerful name for a disaster site. We didn't stop.

In the afternoon we passed through Silverton and the foothills of the Bitterroot Mountains, where we exited the highway at the town of Wallace, which called itself the "Silver Capital of the World." We ate lunch at the Brooks Hotel Restaurant and Lounge.

The restaurant claimed to have a "famous" salad bar, which was, in fact, the most ordinary salad I'd ever encountered. I guess they meant famous, as in, lettuce is famous.

Actually, their claim of fame was unusual. While practically everything in Washington was advertised as "world famous," I noticed that since I'd been in Idaho I hadn't seen a single world-famous shake or burger. Instead, everything in Idaho was "historic." Trees, roads, churches, rocks, mines, just about anything you could attach a sign to.

After lunch we went to the Harvest Grocery Store to stock up on water, fruit, and Gatorade. We were climbing the highway on-ramp when we saw a man standing at the side of the road with his thumb out. He was an older man with a bushy gray beard that fell to the middle of his neck. He wore a train conductor hat, bright yellow-lens sunglasses, and overalls that were striped like the old seersucker suits.

He waved to us. "How y'all?"

"Good afternoon," I said.

"Hey," Kailamai said, looking a little anxious.

"How's the fishing?" I asked.

"Fishing?"

"The hitchhiking," I said.

"Oh," he said with a squint. "Ain't a whole lot of cars coming out of Wallace this time of day. Mind if I walk with you a piece?"

"Not at all."

He ran to the edge of the road and lifted a small canvas pack from the ground, then ran back to catch up with us, much more nimbly than I expected from a man of his years.

"Name's Pete," he said.

"I'm Alan. This is Kailamai."

He tilted his hat. "Ma'am."

"Hey," she said.

"Where y'all be headed?"

"East," I said. "Way east."

Though he walked with us, his thumb was

still extended at his side. "I'm not headed too far. I go to Mullan every week to see my friends."

"You're from Wallace?"

"Most days I am. Seventy years of 'em."

Kailamai walked with her head down, not involving herself in the conversation.

"What do you do in Wallace?" I asked. "For a living?"

"Prospectin' mostly. Some loggin', but mostly prospectin'."

"For gold?"

"Always gold. Well, that ain't entirely true. I've done some silver, but mostly gold."

"Have you had much luck?"

"I always have luck," he said with a slight chuckle. "Just sometimes it's the good kind, sometimes it's the bad kind. More the latter."

"Do you have a family?"

"I did the whole nine yards. My kids live nearby. They keep in touch sometimes."

"Your wife?"

The look on his face was answer enough. "Done with her. Or she done with me. Don't remember which."

"So, in all those years of prospecting, did you ever find the mother lode?"

He swatted at the air in front of him. "Nah. Thought I'd found her a few times, but her milk always dried up."

"How many years have you been looking?"

"About since I was old enough to hold a pan. I'm still lookin'."

"How do you do that?" I asked. "Carry on for seventy years without success."

"Success?" he said. "I'm this side of the dirt, relatively healthy, good friends, kids not in prison, don't know what your definition of success is, but that's mine."

"Of course," I said, feeling the reprimand. "I meant, all those years without finding what you were looking for . . ."

"Ah," he said. "The question is, what would've happened if I found her?" He pointed a bony finger at me. "Worst thing you can give a man is what he wants. The lookin's the thing. When a man gets what he been lookin' for, the road ends, don't it." He smiled. "But you're young. You'll figger it out."

As I thought this over, an old Dodge truck pulled up on the shoulder ahead of us and stopped. "That would be my ride. You wanna lift?"

"No, we're just walking."

"Good day for it. You be safe now, sometimes the loggin' trucks pass a little too close to the shoulders." He opened the passenger side door and climbed in, and the truck sped off.

Most of the day was easy walking, with wide shoulders and plenty of shade. Kailamai and I talked a lot, covering topics as broad as religion

253

to why I had never had a pet dog. And then there were Kailamai's jokes.

"A doctor is talking to his patient one day, and he says, 'I have some bad news and some terrible news.' The patients asks, 'What's the bad news?' and the doctor says, 'You only have twenty-four hours to live.' The patient says, 'Oh no! What news could possibly be worse than that?' And the doctor says, 'I've been trying to contact you since yesterday.' "

Twenty miles or so into our day, we entered Coeur d'Alene National Forest and the roads started climbing again. The roadsides were all inclined and uncampable, and it was getting dark when we reached the state line of Montana and Lookout Pass Ski Resort.

We walked up to the front doors of the resort, but even though there was still some snow on the ground, the lodge was closed for the season. The place looked abandoned, so we pitched our tent behind the main building. I was connecting the last pole on our tent when Kailamai whispered, "Alan."

She was discreetly pointing at a man who was standing near the lodge looking at us.

"What do you think you're doing?" he asked.

I stood up. "Evening," I said.

"You can't camp here," he said gruffly. "It's private property."

I walked toward him. "I'm sorry, but there's no place else around here and it's getting dark. But I promise we'll be gone before anyone else gets here in the morning."

He looked over at Kailamai then back at me. "You're not in trouble with the law, are you?"

Kailamai walked to my side. "No," she said.

"You know we probably wouldn't tell you if we were, but no, we're not. Sorry about trespassing. We would have rented a room, but there was no one here."

"We close on the fifteenth," the man said.

"Please let us camp here," Kailamai said. "I'm really tired. We'll leave early."

The man exhaled audibly, then shook his head. "Grab your packs and come with me."

We left our tent and followed him over to the back of the lodge. He took out a fist of keys and unlocked a door. "You can stay in here. There's no sheets on the beds, but I'm guessing you've got sleeping bags. The bed will be softer than the ground. You can turn the heat up, but turn it back down when you leave."

"Can I pay you something?" I asked.

He shook his head. "No. Just don't break anything and be gone by ten."

"Will do."

"Thank you," Kailamai said. The man turned and walked away. An unexpected kindness. I never even got his name.

CHAPTER
Forty-one

Napoleon said, "My life changed the
day I learned a man would die
for a blue ribbon."
My life changed the day I read that.

Alan Christoffersen's diary

We left the lodge by 8:30 A.M. The road into
Montana was a steep downgrade. At noon we
stopped at Mangold's General Store and Motel
in Haugan. After stocking up on a few supplies,
we walked fifty yards west to the Montana Bar
and Grill. A large black Labrador was lying in
front of the bar's entrance. He didn't move, so
we just stepped over him.

The bar's interior was decorated with bear
and cougar pelts and ram, elk, and deer heads
alongside a bizarre assortment of snowmobile
carcasses. As we entered, Kailamai looked at the
animals and said, "Welcome to the room of
death."

Country music played over the loudspeaker,
accompanied by the whirring electronic sounds
and bells coming from a bank of video poker
games. A fire crackled in a large rock fireplace,

and on the wall behind a green felt pool table a handwritten sign hung:

8 Ball Break. Sink the 8 ball on your break and win the pot.
Bartender must see it to pay out. $1 to play.

There was one man sitting at the bar and one playing video poker. As we entered, the bartender shouted out to us, "Sit anywhere."

We sat down at a table near the front door as the man brought out menus.

"What's good?" I asked.

"House specialty's steamer clams cooked in garlic and white wine. I'll give you a minute to look over your menus. Can I get you a beer?"

"No. I'll just have some water."

"Me too," Kailamai said.

Steamer clams isn't exactly something you'd expect to find in a cowboy bar in northern Montana, but the clams turned out to be quite good, and I finished an entire plate of them. Kailamai ordered a bowl of tomato soup and a grilled cheese sandwich.

As we were finishing our meals, Kailamai said, "I've been meaning to ask you something."

"Go ahead."

"The other night, when you pulled the gun on those guys, why did you point it at the skinny kid? He was the only one who wasn't doing anything to me."

"Psychology," I said.

She squinted. "Psychology?"

"It's like this. A man will die for his honor. If I take aim at the ringleader, he either looks like a coward or he takes a chance and makes me shoot him—both bad scenarios. If I point it at the other two guys, they're feeling intense peer pressure from the ringleader, so again, they might do something stupid and I would have to shoot them.

"The skinny kid had already proved that he didn't want any part of it, so by picking him, the other three can save face, feel like heroes for saving their friend, and walk away. You've got to give people a way out, or else the circumstances will take over."

"Man, you're smart. Did you really think of all that that quickly?"

"No. Actually the skinny kid was the closest. I figured I probably wouldn't miss him."

Kailamai started laughing. "You're such a dork."

We finished eating and stepped back over the dog on our way out.

"Montana reminds you that the Wild West still exists," I said.

Kailamai said, "Wait until you see Wyoming."

We put in 27 miles that day, walking through beautiful, raw country.

About five miles past Haugan we passed a sign that read HISTORIC TREE NURSERY. It wasn't the historic part I found odd so much as the idea of the nursery itself in the middle of a forest. A tree nursery in this land of endless forest is like claiming a saltwater lake in the middle of the ocean.

"Maybe that's why it's historic," Kailamai said. "Did I tell you the one about the duck?"

I shook my head. "I don't think so."

"A duck walks into a drugstore and asks for a tube of ChapStick. The cashier says to the duck, 'That'll be $1.49.' The duck replies, 'Put it on my bill.' "

I think I laughed for about five minutes.

CHAPTER
Forty-two

There are two kinds of suffering in this life. That which pursues us and that which we doggedly pursue.

Alan Christoffersen's diary

The next week of walking took us through St. Regis, Clark Fork, Missoula, Drummond, and Phosphate on our way to Butte.

With each day spent together Kailamai and I grew more comfortable with each other, and though she opened up more to me, she still never talked about her past, which I grew a little more curious about each day.

There weren't many amenities along this stretch, and we camped every night in our tent except for the night at Clark Fork, where we had an unexpected dinner invitation next to a river at a fishing area called St. John's. The sign at the entrance specified,

No Overnight Camping

The sign below it named and showed fish that could be found in the river:

Bull Trout, Rainbow Trout, Brown Trout, Westslope Cutthroat Trout

Around twilight we took a slight detour from the road, and we were walking down by the river when a man stuck his head out the back door of a camper.

"Have you eaten yet?"

I looked over. "Excuse me?"

"Have you eaten yet?"

"No."

"Come on, then. I'm just putting it on."

Kailamai looked at me and I shrugged. "I guess it's time to eat," I said.

The man opened his camper door for us to enter. "Watch your step," he said. He took Kailamai's hand and helped her up.

I followed after her, shutting the narrow door behind me. The camper was comfortable, not old but well used, set in the back of a Ford pickup truck. It had a refrigerator, stereo, television, gas stove and oven, a Formica-topped table, and several cushions on which to sit or sleep.

Our host was tall, maybe a few inches over 6 feet, with thinning reddish-brown hair. He was dressed as an outdoorsman, wearing a flannel shirt and a fishing vest with fishing flies attached.

"I'm frying up some rainbow and brown," he said. "I pulled my limit this afternoon, so there's plenty to eat. Make yourself at home, there's room around the table."

"Sounds good," I said, trying to look amiable. I could tell that Kailamai didn't know what to make of the situation or our host.

The man knew his way around a fish, deboning them with his pocketknife with such ease, I guessed he could have done it blindfolded.

Watching him reminded me of some time back when McKale brought home a trout from the neighborhood Safeway. My father wasn't an outdoorsman, and he never took me fishing or hunting, so I wasn't sure what to do with the fish.

"I thought you were a Boy Scout," McKale said.

"A long, long time ago," I said, adding, "in a galaxy far, far away. And I never had to debone a fish."

"Didn't you camp in the wilderness?" she asked.

"Yes."

"What did you eat?"

"Mostly Pop-Tarts," I replied.

"Figures," she said.

The man sliced a raw fish cleanly down its gut, then flapped back one side of it and peeled out the spine with every bone intact. He dropped the waste into a plastic shopping sack hanging from a cabinet doorknob. Then he cut off the fish's head and tail, dropped them in a separate bag, and started on another fish.

"What do you do with those?" Kailamai asked, pointing to the second bag.

"It's for the cats," he said.

When all the fish were filleted, he combined them all in a brown bag filled with pancake batter, shook it up, then laid the fish two at a time in a skillet of boiling grease until they were light brown and crispy. He dished them onto paper plates for us along with some pork and beans.

"You're welcome to eat in here," the man said, opening the camper door. "I prefer to eat outside."

I looked at Kailamai. "I'm cold," she said.

"You can stay inside," I said. "I'll go out."

I took my plate and followed the man out the back of the camper. He was already seated in a fold-up chair facing the river.

"Pull up a chair," he said, motioning to an identical chair leaning against the truck. I flipped it open with one hand, then sat down next to him. I cut into the trout with my fork and took a bite. It was tender inside and sweet. "It's delicious," I said.

"Everything tastes better outdoors," he said.

I took another bite. Living in Seattle, I've eaten at some of the finest seafood restaurants in America, but I've never tasted fish so good. "You know, I didn't catch your name."

"Great isn't it, not getting all mixed up in

names and brands? Just being. Out here, names are superfluous. It's how it should be."

Frankly, I'd always thought names were a pretty good idea, but after his diatribe I didn't dare ask him his name nor offer mine.

He took a pipe from his vest, then a book of matches. He held a lit match over the pipe's bowl and sucked in the flame. When the pipe was lit, he threw the match on the ground, inhaled deeply, then slowly blew it out. He asked, "Have you been walking long?"

"A while. I started in Seattle."

"That is a walk. Where are you going?"

"Key West."

He looked at me skeptically. "Really?"

"Yes, sir."

He sucked on his pipe. "I've spent some time in the Keys fishing marlin. Home of Papa Hemingway, Tennessee Williams, and Jimmy Buffet."

"I take it you do a lot of fishing," I said.

"You might say that."

"Where are you from?"

"In my former life, Queens."

"Queens, New York?" I asked.

He nodded. "How long have you been married?"

"Seven years," I said, wondering how he knew I'd been married.

"Seven, huh? Don't they have laws against marrying minors in Seattle?"

"You mean . . ." Since we weren't using names, I pointed with my thumb to the camper. "She's just a walking buddy. My wife passed away about six months ago."

"Sorry to hear it." He took a long draw on his pipe. "I had a wife once. I lost her too."

That's all he said. After a minute I asked, "She died?"

"Our marriage died." He looked at me. "I murdered it with work."

"Where did you work?"

"I worked for a company called Young and Rubicam."

I didn't expect that. Young and Rubicam is one of the largest and most prestigious advertising agencies in the world. "You were in advertising?"

"You've heard of it then," he said, not looking altogether happy that I had.

"I used to be in advertising myself," I said. "What did you do?"

"Client services, account management, whatever they're calling it these days. I was over the Chanel account."

"That's a huge account."

"A hundred fifty million dollars," he said slowly. "You don't have an account like Chanel, it has you. I was always gone. Anniversaries, neighborhood parties, birthdays, my father-in-law's funeral. My wife became a stranger. I could tell you precisely what perfumes American women were wearing, in any city in America, in any demographic. But I couldn't tell you what kind of flowers my wife liked. I couldn't even tell you what kind of perfume she liked.

"One day I came home early from a business trip and found her with another man. He was terrified. I'm sure he thought I was going to kill him in a jealous rage. He said, 'I didn't know she was married. Honest.' My wife said, 'Then you've got something in common with my husband.' " He shook his head. "I've got to hand it to her, that was pretty clever under the circumstances. She always had a quick wit."

I wasn't sure what to say.

"We divorced, of course. I quit my job, bought this truck, and started fishing." He set his plate on the ground. "I'm guessing your wife never wanted to leave."

I looked out over the river. "No, she would have stayed." I turned back to him. "Did you ever try to fix things with your wife?"

"When I got over my rage, I asked her to stay. I even told her I'd quit my job. But it was too late."

"I had a small agency in Seattle. I worked a lot too, but my wife was involved. At least as much as she cared to be."

"That couldn't happen at a big agency," he said.

"No, it couldn't," I agreed.

266

He blew out a cloud of smoke. "I think I was addicted to the stress."

"I've seen that happen," I said. "Stress is like a drug. It will kill you as well." I looked at him. "That's why you fish."

"That's why I fish." He took another long draw on his pipe, then let it out slowly. "What are you going to do when you reach Key West?"

"I don't know. Eat some key lime pie."

He started laughing, almost imperceptibly at first, then it grew until he almost doubled over. "Key lime pie," he said. "Eat some key lime pie."

By the time we finished eating, it was dark.

"Thank you for dinner," I said. "We better get going. We still need to make camp."

"Where are you camping tonight?" he asked.

"I'm not sure. The first campground we come to."

"That will be a while," he said. "There's nothing around here. You're welcome to stay with me. There's a couple bunk beds in back. I can sleep up in the cabin."

"I thought there was no overnight camping."

"I'm not camping," he said. "I'm parking."

Spun like an adman, I thought.

I slept in a bunk that hung over the truck's cabin and Kailamai slept on cushions above the table. She was still a little apprehensive about our host, and after I turned out the lights she whispered to me, "You don't think he's like a serial killer or something, do you?"

"No," I whispered back. "Worse."

"What?"

"He's an adman."

I was just about asleep when Kailamai said, "Two muffins are in an oven and one says to the other, 'Sure is hot in here.' The other shouts, 'Holy cow, a talking muffin!' "

CHAPTER
Forty-three

It would appear that a significant portion of the Montana state budget has gone to the making of historical markers.

Alan Christoffersen's diary

The adman (he never told us his name) made breakfast for us, a homemade concoction he called scramble-mamble, a potpourri of diced potatoes, eggs, cheddar cheese, trout, onions, and bacon. It was actually pretty good.

We thanked him, wished him well, and headed off toward Missoula.

"That guy liked to fish," Kailamai said.

"Everyone needs a reason to get up in the morning," I said.

The traffic grew heavier as we neared Missoula, and I fully expected we'd be stopped by the Highway Patrol, but it never happened. As we exited toward the town, we passed a billboard advertising the "Testicle Festival."

"What do you think that is?" Kailamai asked.

"I don't want to know," I said.

Later that afternoon we stopped at a gas-station convenience store for water and a Hostess apple pie for Kailamai. As we came out of the store, we walked past a large semi filling up at the gas pumps. A trucker sat on the front bumper of his truck.

"Howdy," he said to us with a subtle tip of his cap. He wore a flannel shirt and a belt buckle the size of a pancake.

"Could you tell us where's the next hotel?" I asked.

"Depends on which way you're goin'. East or west?"

"East."

"Maybe thirty miles."

I groaned. "Thanks." I turned away.

"Need a ride? I'm headed that way."

"No thanks. We're walking."

"Okay. Be safe now."

The truckers were always helpful.

A couple hours later I said, "I've discovered something."

"What?" Kailamai asked.

"There's a secret to naming Montana towns. You pick an animal and then one of its body parts, and combine them."

She looked at me like I was crazy.

"No, really, think about it. We've been through Beaver Tail, Bearmouth, Bull's Eye—the possibilities are endless."

"I could be good at this," Kailamai said. "We could name the next town Moose Antler."

"Totally believable," I said. "Or Otter Tail."

"Rabbit's Foot."

"Badger Paw."

"Wait," Kailamai said, "I've got the best one. Monkey Butt, Montana."

We both started laughing. I liked this girl.

The next town we came to didn't conform to my name formula—Drummond—but the first restaurant we passed did. The Bull's End Café. A sign in front of the eatery proclaimed PAULINE'S BBQ SAUCE MADE HERE beneath the backside of an anatomically correct bull. Not surprisingly, the establishment was out of business.

"That's just gross," Kailamai said. "What part of that is supposed to make you want to eat there?"

"That's why there are advertising agencies," I said.

A little further down the road we came to the Frosty Freeze, a weathered A-framed building with a sliding window for takeout. Out in front of the building there was a plywood, painted pig holding an American flag under a sign that advertised ITALIAN SLOPPY JOE'S, *YOU'LL LOVE 'EM!*

The place looked abandoned, but there was a WE ARE OPEN paper sign on the window. As soon as we approached the building, a woman appeared at the counter.

"What can I get for you?" she asked, her breath

still pungent from the cigarette I could see smoking behind her.

"I'll try your Italian sloppy joe," I said. "How about you, Kailamai?"

"I'll have the sloppy joe too. Can I have Tater Tots?"

"We'll have Tots on both and a Diet Coke for me."

"We have Pepsi products," she said.

"Fine, a Diet Pepsi and a Sprite for her."

"We don't have Sprite, we have Pepsi products."

"Whatever looks like Sprite," I said.

"Sierra Mist," she said, leaving the window to prepare our meals.

The special turned out to be a sloppy joe with the addition of provolone cheese, onions, and garlic, which was surprisingly good, though Kailamai picked out the onions.

That night we pitched our tent near a golf course.

"Do you golf?" Kailamai asked.

"I used to," I said, rolling out my sleeping bag.

"This man was out golfing with his buddies. He was about to putt when a hearse drove by leading a funeral procession. The man set down his club, took off his hat, and put it over his heart until the procession had passed. 'That was the most decent thing I've ever seen you do,' one of his friends said.

" 'It's the least I could do,' he replied. 'We were married thirty-two years.' "

CHAPTER
Forty-four

Today I learned Kailamai's story.
It's almost as difficult to believe that
someone with so many trials could
harbor such hope, as that there are
those with so much advantage
who harbor such hopelessness.

Alan Christoffersen's diary

The next morning the river that had intermittently followed our journey was running alongside us again. I don't know why the sound of the river made me feel peaceful—I've heard it has something to do with our experience in the womb—but few things so easily bring calm as the sound of rushing water.

Perhaps that had something to do with why it was here, along that barren stretch of highway, that Kailamai finally told me her story. We had been walking quietly for a few minutes when she said, "You haven't said anything about your mother."

"She passed away when I was eight."

"Do you remember what she was like?"

"She was lovely," I said. "She was the kindest person I've ever known. Once I saw her give some money to a guy begging on the street. My dad got real mad at her. He said, 'You know he's just going to use it to buy booze.' My mother said, 'Maybe that's what he needs most right now.'

"If the world was populated with people like her, there would be no wars or want." I frowned. "I miss her. After all this time I still miss her."

"I wish I had a mother like that," Kailamai said. She bowed her head and we walked a ways in silence. Then she asked, "Do you want to know why I was put in foster care?"

"If you want to tell me."

"It's kind of a long story."

"We've got a long walk," I said.

"Okay." She took a deep breath. "My mother was the opposite of yours. She was really abusive. Actually, both my mother and my older sister were. Growing up, I thought that getting beaten up was part of life. My sister beat me up almost every day, and my mother would beat the tar out of me at least once a week. Once she beat me so badly that it took me more than an hour before I could even crawl back to my room."

I now understood why she wasn't sorry her mother was dead. "What was wrong with them that they thought they could beat you?" I asked.

"I don't know." She pulled her hair back from her face. "Probably because they could. I was smaller than them and they were just mean.

274

They never, like said, 'Pardon me,' or stuff like that, they'd just shove you out of the way or pull you by your hair.

"It wasn't until the fourth grade that I realized that not everyone had a home like mine. I couldn't believe that some of my classmates actually liked their parents."

"That's remarkably sad," I said.

"My mom was an alcoholic. She lived off welfare and food stamps and whatever men gave her. When I got a little older, the men my mother brought home started noticing me. Every few months one of them would come at me. I knew my mother knew what they were doing, but she just acted like it was no big deal. Then my mother married one of them and he moved in. Kurt," she said, her mouth twisting a little with the name.

"Kurt was a meth addict and he got my mom and sister on it. I wouldn't do drugs, so he hated me. Once my sister was beating me up, and he sat there and cheered her on. It was the worst whupping she'd ever given me.

"He'd hit me too. But it wasn't like he was mad, it's like it turned him on or something. He'd get mad at me for stupid things, like he'd say I didn't change the toilet paper roll, and so I was going to get it. He liked to make it last. Once he made me sit in the garage and wait a whole hour for him to beat me. Usually, he'd

275

make me pull my pants down so he could beat my bare butt."

"Why didn't you tell anyone?"

She kicked a stone. "It's not that easy," she said. "When it's all you know, you just accept it."

I frowned.

"But school was good. When I got to middle school, my life changed. I had this really great history teacher who liked me. Mrs. Duncan. She told me how smart I was. Once I got the highest score on a test, and she held up my test and told the whole class. She even gave me her cell phone number and said I could call her any time I had a question. I never did, but it was cool that I could have.

"Then one day, just before school got out, the school nurse called me down to her office. She started asking me about the bruises on my arm. I told her I fell down the stairs.

"Then she asked me about my mother. I was really scared and I told her that everything was good at home, but she knew I was lying. Finally, after like a whole hour of questions, I just broke down and told her everything. She listened and took notes. When I was done talking, she said, 'I want you to go home and pack a suitcase. Someone will come get you.'

"She never said *who* was coming. So I walked home wondering what was going to happen. When I walked in the house, my mother was furious. She said that I had left a mess in the kitchen and she went after me. I never ran from her anymore, it only made her madder, so I just stood there while she hit me.

"When she was done, I had a bloody nose and was lying on the floor, and she kicked me in the butt and told me to clean up the blood I'd gotten on the carpet and then go to my room. I wiped up my blood and then, when I was going to my room, she said something that hurt worse than the beating. She said, 'Why did you have to be born?'

"I just kind of flipped. I said, 'You don't have to worry about me anymore. Someone's coming to take me away.'

"She started laughing. She said, 'Who would want a little turd like you?'

"It was like a miracle because just then someone rang the doorbell. My mother looked at the door, then me, then back at the door. She was, like, frozen. They pounded on the door, then a man shouted, 'Open the door. Police.' My mother opened it. There were six police officers. It was really scary. Two of them got in my mother's face and began shouting at her, and another one walked over to me. I thought he was going to shout at me too, but he didn't. He asked, 'Are you Kailamai?' I said, 'Yes.' He said, 'Go upstairs and pack up your things.'

"I ran upstairs and threw everything I had in a pillow case and brought it down.

"When I came back downstairs, the police officer said, 'If you want, you can say goodbye to your mother.' I went over to hug my mother, but she wouldn't have anything to do with me. The policeman got really mad and said, 'Hug your daughter!' She hugged me, but it was only because she was afraid. As we were walking out, I started to cry, and I looked back at her and she said, 'You're the devil's child.' One of the policemen said, 'Then that makes you the devil. We'll deal with you later.' They put me in the back of the police car."

"That must have been frightening," I said.

"It was. I mean, the policeman was nice and all. He asked me what radio station I liked. But I was still really scared. I thought I was going to jail. Instead he drove me up into the mountains where there were two other cars parked. A tall, redheaded woman came out of one. She was my caseworker. Then a woman and her daughter came out of the other. Lois and Mabel Thompson. They were my first foster home. I was like their twentieth kid, so they knew what they were doing. They were really nice.

"After a year and a half the state sent me back to my mom. The courts made her take classes about how to be a decent mother and she was all honey and sugar when they brought me back.

That lasted for about two hours, then she went back to her old self. Just before I went to bed, she smacked me in the head and told me she had gotten into all kinds of trouble because of me and I was going to pay for it.

"The next day her husband took me out to the garage and made me take my pants off, then he whipped me with his belt. A neighbor heard me scream and called the police. They came and got me right away. They took me to this place called Children's Village. I was there for a few months, except when I was sent to a mental hospital."

"Why were you sent to a mental hospital?" I asked.

"Because I sent a letter to my judge that said if he sent me back to my mother I would commit suicide. He didn't like that very much."

I looked at her gravely. "Would you have?"

"Maybe. I was thinking about it. After the mental hospital they sent me to live with this couple named David and Karlynne. They were nice. I was the first foster child they'd ever had, so everything was kind of harder for them. Karlynne had a job and had to travel a lot, which meant I had to be home alone with her husband. David never did anything bad to me, but I didn't really trust men, so I told her that I was afraid of being left alone with him for a week. But she had to work, so she left, and the second day I freaked out and called my caseworker and they came and got me."

"You don't seem uncomfortable with me," I said.

"You're different."

"How am I different?"

"I don't know. I just like you."

"I like you too," I said. "So what happened next?"

"After that they changed my caseworker. My new caseworker was awful. She didn't believe that my mother was as bad as I told everyone, so she filed to have me sent back home. I told her that I would commit suicide and she just said I was manipulative and knew how to work the system. I didn't like her at all. I called her supervisor and they changed her."

I asked, "How old were you then?"

"It wasn't too long ago. Maybe six months. While the state was trying to decide what to do with me, my mother gave up all her custodial rights to me. The weird thing is, she died a week later." She looked at me. "True story."

"What did she die from?"

"I don't know. She was really fat and had diabetes and high blood pressure, so they just said natural causes. But honestly, I think her husband killed her. No one knows—there wasn't one of those things they do to see why you died."

"An autopsy?"

"Yeah," she said. "An autopsy." She put her hands in her pockets. "They put me back at the group home for a while. Then they sent me to a new foster family, the Brysons. But they were really strict and negative and I just couldn't do it, so one day while Mrs. Bryson was grocery shopping I ran away. I've been on the streets ever since."

"Which brings you to where I met you," I said.

She nodded. "Pretty unbelievable life, huh?"

"What's unbelievable to me is how you've managed to remain so positive. I've been with you for more than a week, and you haven't complained once."

She smiled. "I heard someone say, 'There's no problem so big that whining won't make it worse.' "

I laughed.

"The way I see it," she said, "everyone has problems. It's how you choose to deal with them. Some people choose to be whiners, some choose to be winners. Some choose to be victims, some choose to be victors."

I put my hand on her shoulder. "You're the type who thinks of the glass as being half full instead of half empty."

"No," she said, "I'm just grateful for the glass."

I smiled. "Out of the mouth of babes," I said, "out of the mouth of babes."

CHAPTER
Forty-five

There are times when the great cosmic architect gives us brief glimpses of the blueprint so we can do our part.

Alan Christoffersen's diary

Two days later we walked into Butte, Montana, which has the coolest city sign I'd ever seen— an old mining rig strung with white lights.

Butte's a first-rate town, with movie theaters and shopping malls and at least a dozen hotels to choose from. I chose the Hampton Inn, and at the recommendation of the hotel clerk, Kailamai and I ate dinner at a nearby steakhouse called the Montana Club.

We were waiting for our main entrées when I was struck by a flash of genius. It must have shown on my face because Kailamai gave me a puzzled look. "What?"

"Nothing," I said.

"Why are you looking at me like that?"

"I was just thinking," I said vaguely. "So let me ask you something. If you could suddenly have any life at all, what would it look like?"

"You mean, like, if I could be queen of the world or Britney Spears?"

I grinned. "I was thinking of something a little more realistic."

She thought about my question. "Well, since this is fantasy and I could have anything, I'd live in a nice home near a college where I could go to school to be a lawyer. The home doesn't need to be a mansion, just a nice place that smells good.

"I wouldn't want to be treated like a foster child anymore, but I'd still want to live with someone who was a little older so she could teach me things that people with normal lives already know. But she would still be fun and joke and stuff and not bust my chops all the time. Someone like you."

"I'm no fun," I said.

"See, you're always joking," she replied. "And we'd go to a movie now and then or bowling or hiking. And I'd go to school and work a job and also I would help out around the house, because I wouldn't want my roommate to think I was a freeloader."

"Are you sure that's really what you want?" I asked.

"That would be heaven."

"What if I could make it happen?"

She looked at me curiously. "Then I'd say you were an angel or something."

"An angel, huh?" I got up from the table. "I need to make a call."

■ ■ ■

We slept in the next morning, a rare luxury. We showered and dressed, then went downstairs for the complimentary breakfast.

"Yellowstone awaits," Kailamai said, spreading cream cheese over a bagel. "Ready to hit the road?"

"No. Not today."

"No?"

"We've been putting in a lot of miles lately. I thought we should take a day off. Have a play day."

Her face lit with excitement. "Really?"

"I think we deserve it. We should go bowling, have a nice lunch, maybe go shopping."

Her smile grew. "Sounds awesome."

"I hope you don't mind, but a friend of mine's going to join us."

"You have a friend in Butte?"

"No, she actually lives in Spokane. She's driving all the way here."

"Is she like a girlfriend?"

"No, just a good friend."

"When is she coming?"

"She should be here any minute."

I was getting directions from the clerk at the front desk to the nearest bowling alley when Nicole walked into the lobby. She smiled when she saw me. "Alan!"

We embraced. "It's good to see you," I said. It

had only been eighteen days, but it already felt like a year since I'd left Spokane.

Nicole looked around the hotel lobby. "Where is she?"

"Kailamai, come here," I said, waving her over. "Meet my friend."

Kailamai had been watching our reunion. She set her pancakes down and walked over.

"This is my friend, Nicole," I said.

"Hello," Kailamai said, sounding uncharacteristically formal. "It's nice to meet you."

"It's nice meeting you too," Nicole said. "Alan's told me a lot about you."

"Good things I hope."

"All good," Nicole said. "Do you mind me hanging out with you guys today?"

"No problem."

Nicole turned to me. "So what's on the agenda?"

"I think some bowling might be in order," I said.

Nicole asked Kailamai, "Do you like to bowl?"

"Who doesn't?" Kailamai said.

"Then let's go bowling," Nicole said.

Kailamai looked back and forth between us. "If you two would rather just be alone . . ."

"Absolutely not," I said.

Nicole shook her head. "Sorry, you're stuck with us."

Kailamai smiled. "Good, sounds fun."

We climbed into Nicole's Malibu and drove a few miles to Kingpin Lanes. We were all pretty bad bowlers and our combined scores wouldn't equal a decent IQ, but that only added to the fun.

After one throw Kailamai said, "What does one of my bowling balls and a drunk have in common?"

"What?" I said.

"Chances are they'll both end up in the gutter."

Afterward we walked through a mall, and Nicole and Kailamai went off clothes shopping while I browsed a bookstore and then sat in the courtyard to read a magazine and drink an Orange Julius. An hour later they found me.

"Look what Nicole bought me," Kailamai said excitedly, holding up a denim jacket with white stitching and rhinestones. "This cool coat."

"She picked it out," Nicole said. "She's got great taste. She helped me find the perfect pair of jeans."

I smiled. They had already connected. After the mall we headed back over to the Montana Club for lunch.

Nicole got a phone call on our way into the restaurant and stayed out in the restaurant's lobby while Kailamai and I sat down at our table.

"So what do you think of Nicole?" I asked.

"You two should get married."

I smiled wryly. "That's not what I meant."

"I think she's really cool. She should go to Yellowstone with us."

"No, she's got to get back to school."

Kailamai looked disappointed.

A few minutes later Nicole entered the dining room and sat down in a chair next to Kailamai, across from me.

"Everything okay?" I asked.

"It was my sister," she said, rolling her eyes. "She calls a lot now." She turned to Kailamai. "So what's good?"

"I had the French dip and sweet potato fries last night," Kailamai said. "They were both awesome. I'm going to try making those fries some day."

"You can cook?" Nicole asked.

"A few things. I make a mean grilled cheese sandwich and I can make pizza dough. I thought of being a chef once. That or a judge."

Nicole laughed. "You have diverse tastes."

"Well, in both cases, you have to make sure things are done right."

"You're right," Nicole said, "you're absolutely right."

The waitress came and took our orders and then Kailamai left to use the restroom. When she was gone, I said, "So, what do you think?"

Nicole smiled. "I think she's great. I think it's a great idea."

"What if it doesn't work out?"

Nicole nodded. "We'll cross that bridge when we come to it—if we ever do. But I'm not worried. I have a good feeling about her. It will be nice having company again."

"Do you want to ask her or should I?"

"Maybe you should."

A few minutes later Kailamai returned. After she sat down, I said to her, "Remember our talk last night, when you told me about your perfect world?"

She put her napkin on her lap. "Yeah."

"Did you mean it?"

She looked at me quizzically. "Yeah, I mean, it was just wishful thinking, but I hope that something like that happens someday."

"Well, someday is today."

She looked back and forth between us. "What do you mean?"

"Nicole didn't drive all this way just to go bowling. She came to meet you."

Kailamai looked at Nicole. "Why would you do that?"

"Because," I said, "Nicole's your perfect world. She's smart and fun, she lives less than a mile from Gonzaga University, and she's willing to take you in as her roommate, pay for your room, and help you get into school, as long as you get good grades, help out around the house, and are respectful."

Kailamai's eyes darted back and forth between both of us. "Are you kidding me?"

"What do you think?" Nicole asked.

After a moment she said, "It's like a dream come true." She turned to Nicole. "Why would you do that? You don't even know me."

"No, but I know Alan and I trust him."

Kailamai's eyes welled up. "I can't believe this."

The waiter brought our food. After he was gone, I said, "There is one catch."

"What's that?" Kailamai asked.

"You need to leave this afternoon. Nicole's headed back to Spokane as soon as we finish lunch."

Kailamai looked surprised. "But . . . Yellowstone."

"Yellowstone's not going anywhere," I said.

She looked down at her food. "Wow, for once I'm not hungry."

"So what's your decision?" Nicole asked.

A big smile crossed her lips. "Yes. Thank you. Yes."

We finished eating, then Nicole drove us back to the hotel. I stayed in the lobby with Nicole while Kailamai ran upstairs to get her things.

"Remember what I said to you the day you left?" Nicole asked. "The happiest I've ever been was when I was taking care of someone." She smiled at me. "Once again, you've changed my life."

"Well, no one deserves a chance more than Kailamai. She's lucky to have a mentor like you. She'll go far."

A big smile crossed Nicole's face. "Thank you."

A few minutes later Kailamai came into the lobby carrying her backpack.

"Ready?" I asked.

"Yeah."

We went outside and I put her bag in the Malibu's trunk.

"I'm going to miss walking with you," Kailamai said.

I looked at her fondly. "Me too. Be a good roommate. And a good judge or chef. Make me proud."

"I will, I promise." She looked down. "Will I ever see you again?"

"Absolutely."

She hugged me, then she turned to Nicole.

"Let's go, roomie." She climbed into the car.

Nicole walked up and hugged me. "Another goodbye. It was hard enough the first time."

"I hate goodbye," I said. "How about I just say, 'See you later.'"

"Promise?"

"I promise. I'll call to see how things are going."

"I'll look forward to it." She was starting to tear up, so she quickly kissed my cheek, then climbed into the car and started it. "Bye," she said sweetly.

"Goodbye," I said.

Kailamai waved as they drove off.

"Alone again," I said. I took a deep breath, then went up to my room and took a long, hot bath.

CHAPTER
Forty-six

I'm alone again. It's not that I
dislike the company, it's just that
I've already heard all his stories.

Alan Christoffersen's diary

The next morning I went downstairs for breakfast—Raisin Bran with skim milk, a banana, and
a glass of orange juice. At the table next to me
was a man wearing a lanyard that read HI, MY
NAME IS TONY written in blue marker. He
was watching ESPN on the television mounted
on the dining room wall.

"Excuse me," I said. "Do you know the fastest
way from here to Highway 2?"

He turned to me. "Sure. Just turn right in front
of the hotel and keep going south about two
miles down to the MT2 sign. You can't miss it."

"Thank you."

"Where are you headed?"

"I'm walking to Yellowstone."

"You're walking all the way to Yellowstone?"

"Actually, I'm walking to Key West."

"Florida?"

"Yes."

He looked at me for a moment, then said, "Man, I wish I were doing that."

I was on the road by eight. I already missed Kailamai. I missed her spirit. I even missed her jokes.

Outside of Butte, I got on Highway 2 toward Whitehall. The next three days took me through the towns of Silver Star, Twin Bridges, and Sheridan. Silver Star was a small but legitimate town. It had a scrap metal yard, a taxidermist, and a stop called Granny's Country Store with a sign outside that said FREE COFFEE, WEDNESDAY–SATURDAY, 10–6.

I stopped at the store, where I picked up a wilderness survival book and a pamphlet that claimed it would help me predict the weather using the wisdom of our forefathers. The small book was filled with chestnuts like:

When the dew is on the grass,
Rain will never come to pass.
When grass is dry at morning light,
Look for rain before the night!

And (according to the book) the single most useful weather proverb of all:

Red Sky at night,
Sailor's delight.

Red sky in the morning,
Sailors take warning!

I filled up my canteen from the bathroom sink, bought some honeycomb, and chose two cellophane-wrapped sandwiches from a refrigerator. I learned that the woman who ran the store was the owner, which, I guess, technically made her Granny. She was probably in her late thirties, had long, brunette hair that fell to her waist, and didn't wear shoes on the hardwood floor.

I passed Jefferson Camp (where the Lewis and Clark expedition had camped), then a few miles later crossed the Jefferson River and followed the Lewis and Clark Trail all the way to the town of Twin Bridges.

Twin Bridges bills itself as "The Small City That Cares." The town had GO FALCON signs posted in most of the store windows. I ate dinner at the Wagon Wheel Restaurant, which was surprisingly crowded, and bought supplies at the Main Street Market.

I spent the night at King's Motel, which had a sign outside proclaiming AWARD WINNING ROOMS, which was infinitely better than "world famous" or "historic." I was skeptical of the claim until the owner—a fishing outfitter named Don who looked like Ernest Hemingway in shorts—gave me a tour of the place. The rooms were cozy, wood paneled cabins with kitchenettes. The cost was just $73 a night, and as a bonus, Don offered to take me fly-fishing in the morning. I told him I'd have to pass on the fishing, but rented one of his rooms.

Sheridan was only eight miles from Twin Bridges, and most of the terrain between them was smooth, with green meadows and grazing sheep. Sheridan was larger than the last three towns I'd passed through and had a bank and a Napa Auto Parts Store alongside the Ruby Saloon, which had a sign advertising BOOZED BUNS, which I mused was either a bread product infused with alcohol, or referred to the help.

I stopped at the Sheridan Bakery & Café and ordered a ham and cheese roll and a cinnamon bun. Next to my table was a sign on the wall that read:

We have the right to refuse service to anyone at any time. No exceptions, Steve, Joe, and Allen

A whiteboard mounted to the wall across from my table read:

**TRIVIA QUESTION:
Where is the Trevi Fountain located?**

Someone had scrawled beneath it: "Trevi?"

Whoever answered the questions correctly got a free maple bar, which I hope hadn't been made especially for the contest, since the sign had been posted a month earlier and still no one had won. I asked the manager, a woman named Francie, if I could give it a shot.

"Sure thing, honey. Where is the Trevi Fountain?" she asked with the intensity of a game show host.

McKale and I had been to Rome twice on advertising incentive trips, and I was quite familiar with the beautiful fountain of Neptune that capped the end of the ancient Roman aqueducts.

"The Trevi Fountain is just a little east of Via Veneto, about a half mile from the Spanish Steps."

She shook her head. "No," she said sadly. "It's in Italy."

I just smiled. "Well, I tried."

The next day I walked along the Ruby River, which, in the 1860s, was originally called the Stinking Water River by the miners. Sometime later it was renamed the Ruby River after the gems found along its length, which turned out not to be rubies, but garnets.

A sign mounted near the river shared several interesting facts: First, the gold once mined there by dredges was used to finance Harvard University in the early twentieth century. Second, the Ruby River was the site of the Vigilante Trail, and the dreaded numbers 3-7-77 were of historic significance, though it didn't explain why.

The next town I came to, Nevada City, was closed. Literally. Nevada City was an authentic old western town with a music hall, blacksmith shop, barbershop, saloons, and a saddler. The town looked like a movie set—which it was— and outside the village entrance was a long list of all the movies that had been shot on the premises. The numbers 3-7-77 were posted on one of the buildings here as well. *Maybe it was a date,* I thought. March 7, 1877.

Eight miles down the road was Christine City, which was also an Old West town, and more authentic than Nevada City though not as colorful. Fortunately for me, it was open. I stopped in a small tourist shop to browse, and I asked the shop's proprietor the meaning of 3-7-77. She seemed glad for the question.

"If you had that number placed in your yard by the vigilantes, you had 3 days, 7 hours, and 77 minutes to get out of town or you would be buried in a grave 3 feet wide, 7 feet long, and 77 inches deep. However, some believe that those numbers were also connected to the local Masonic order, who in the 1860s had 3 deacons, 7 elders, and 77 members."

The woman told me that their town had a "boot hill," which is where the vigilantes' victims were buried, placed in graves with their boots pointing away from the sun.

I ate lunch at a small restaurant called the Outlaw Café. When I asked the waitress, Cora, if their food was any good, she replied, "Oh, it's good all right. Before I worked here I looked like Twiggy, now look at me." She spun around, modeling her plump physique for me.

I told her about my walk, and she said another man had walked through Christine City on his way across the country—Tim. "He carries a cross with him." She gave him extra tea bags and sugar packets to help keep him warm in the winter.

I kind of hated leaving the town. I walked until dark and spent the night in the city of Ennis, which, no matter how many times I read the name, didn't seem right.

The next two days were some of the dullest walking I'd encountered yet on my journey. The view came with two options—flat, dull landscape with trees or flat, dull landscape without. The roads were smooth, with wide shoulders but no coverage from the elements. The only excitement was when someone threw a plastic cup filled with soda at me from a speeding car.

Seven days from Butte, I entered the Gallatin National Forest, Earthquake Lake Geologic Area.

The lake had a surreal quality. The water was

thick with moss and the tops of dead trees poked out of its surface like stubble, some even in the center of the lake. A mile or two past the entry there was an observation point with a plaque:

On Aug. 17, 1959, a 7.5 earthquake triggered a massive landslide. 80 million tons of rock— half the mountain—fell, creating this lake, now 4 miles long and 120 feet deep.

That explained the trees in the middle of the lake. The next day I reached West Yellowstone.

CHAPTER
Forty-seven

The last time I was in Yellowstone
I was wearing Superman underwear.

Alan Christoffersen's diary

When I was seven years old, my family took a trip to Yellowstone National Park (the same trip my father and I had talked about at the IHOP). That was years ago, a unique era, when America's love affair with the car was on a par with our old fear of beeping Russian satellites. There was a remarkable, though admittedly charming, naïveté to our perception of the park —almost a collective suspension of reality in our national imagination. Yellowstone was just a grand, outdoor stage show with animal actors conveniently placed for our entertainment— moose were gawking, Bullwinkle creatures, and bears were domesticated fur balls with names like Yogi and Boo-Boo, who loved picnic baskets and tourists and were more than happy to pose for photographs. It has taken more than a few grisly maulings to alter our collective paradigm. Wild animals are, well, wild.

While my mother was standing in line at the restroom near the Old Faithful Inn, my father and I watched a tourist (I remember her looking like a larger version of Lucille Ball) walk up to a wild buffalo for a prized photo op, her husband, eyeing her through the lens piece of a Brownie camera, verbally nudging her: "Just a little closer, Madge. Yes, just a few steps more. Yes! Like that! Put your hand up, yeah, rub its neck."

The buffalo looked at her through glassy eyes roughly the size of tennis balls like she was the stupidest creature on God's green earth (possibly true), trying to decide whether to walk away in disgust or trample her for the ultimate good of the human gene pool.

My dad watched the scene unfold with a curious, mixed expression of amusement and envy. Ultimately, the buffalo didn't do anything but walk away. Sometimes nature takes compassion on stupidity.

I don't know what self-talk might take place in a buffalo's brain, but I imagine it went something like this, "These guys are really at the top of the food chain?"

Like so much of life, the anticipation of that trip was even better than the trip itself. A few weeks before our vacation my mother took me to the Buster Brown shoe store to buy some new Keds—green canvas boat shoes with white-trimmed soles—and a new T-shirt with a picture of Charlie Brown running at a football held by

Lucy. (Digression: why, oh why, didn't Charles Schulz let Charlie Brown kick the football in his last comic strip—what hope he could have left humanity!)

We were in the car for a length of time that, to my young mind, seemed the equivalent of my entire second-grade year, but in the end it was all worth it. Being an only child, I was denied the pleasure of fighting with a sibling (He's on my side of the car. He stuck his tongue out at me! He touched me first.), but on the plus side, I did have the entire back seat to lie down on.

We owned a candy-apple red Ford Galaxy 500, a car slightly larger than a sand barge, with considerably worse mileage. I remember once we were climbing a hill and my father pointed to the gas gauge and said, "Watch this." He pressed down on the gas pedal and the gas needle visibly dropped a point or two.

My father was uncharacteristically generous on that trip, and I was allowed, actually encouraged, to purchase a souvenir. I chose a ceramic bear with fuzz painted on all the right places, and a box that had a wood-burned sketch of Old Faithful. I remember the agonizing internal debate that went on in my young mind between choosing an authentic Indian hand-sewn leather wallet (manufactured in Taiwan) or the box. In the end, the box won out since it had a real lock and key.

My parents and I stood shoulder-to-shoulder with a crowd of tourists at Old Faithful, Yellowstone's most famous geyser. True to its name, the geyser erupted. I remember my father standing there, his hands thrust deep in his back pockets, my mother at his side, holding my hand lest I have the sudden impulse to run and jump on the spray.

Old Faithful is neither the most spectacular nor the highest geyser in the park. What made Old Faithful so famous is its reliability and short window of eruptions. According to NASA (I'm not sure why they cared about such things), from 1870 through 1966 little had changed the geyser's eruption cycle.

Before the feds made laws protecting the site, people would actually throw their laundry inside the geyser, which (I'm told) had a particularly pleasing effect to linen and cotton fabrics but tended to tear woolen garments to shreds.

Actually, Old Faithful's spout is not the kind of thing one sets a watch to, as its eruptions occur at intervals from 45 to 125 minutes apart, which means you could be standing there for two hours to watch a spray that may last only 90 seconds—a fitting analogy for life. I don't remember how long our eruption was; I just remember my father staring at the spout in awe and muttering, "Would you look at that . . ."

If you put a gun to my head, I still couldn't

tell you what it is about water shooting from a hole that would attract millions of tourists. It is the only time in my recollection that water spraying from the ground would warrant anything from my father except a curse and a call to the plumber.

Later that same day we stopped at the Morning Glory Pool. Today that amazing blue pool is fenced off, but back then it wasn't. There was just a little wood-plank path that wound around it. Walking the path terrified me. The water is crystal-clear, and the rock formation underneath looks like an open mouth, so even though the pool is only twenty-three feet deep, it seemed like it dropped to the center of the earth.

As we walked around the pool, I clung to my mother's hand, desperately fearing falling into the water and being lost in its depth. It never occurred to me that at 171.6 degrees, I would be burned into unconsciousness long before I hit bottom.

Today, due to tourist abuse, the pool is mockingly called Fading Glory. The pool's once Windex-blue color has changed from tourists tossing in *tons* of trash (yes, tons), which has blocked the pool's natural vents, lowered its temperature, and upset its balance.

I'm not sure what would possess someone to throw trash into these beautiful pools, let alone tons of it. It's not as if Yellowstone doesn't offer a hundred thousand acres of convenient landfill. "Clyde, dear, will you take the trash and dump it into the pristine crystal pool? Thanks, honey." But then, it never occurred to me to wash my clothes in Old Faithful either. Maybe something's just wrong with me.

I left Yellowstone Park certain that I would someday be a mountainman: traveling the wilderness alone, eating jerky and venison in my fringed, rawhide suit, which, not counting the apparel, wasn't a far cry from where I was today. We should be careful of what we dream of, as apparently life, or God, has a sense of humor.

My father liked to drive at night and I slept for most of the ride home. I still remember the feel and smell of cold vinyl against my face. Somehow I woke in my own bed, the soft white sheets tucked in around me. I miss that. Childhood was magical that way.

I hadn't been back to Yellowstone since.

CHAPTER
Forty-eight

Nothing clears the mind (nor colon),
like an encounter with a Grizzly Bear.

Alan Christoffersen's diary

Prior to entering the park, I spent the night at the Brandin' Iron Inn, which had a large replica of a bear trap over the front doors. The next morning I ate an Egg McMuffin for breakfast, then walked into Yellowstone Park.

Pedestrians, as well as cars, are required to pay an entrance fee and I paid $12, which was valid for seven days. Less than 100 yards past the gate a large sign informed me that I was now in Wyoming.

Just a few miles in, I passed two trumpeter swans in a pond surrounded by trees growing at 30-degree angles. I was happy to be back in nature and feel her healing. That night I pitched my tent in a place called Whiskey Flats.

The next morning's walk led me past the Midway Geyser Basin and Biscuit Basin, where I watched the steaming geyser water run down fluted, sandstone gullies to cool in the river.

An hour later a sign told me Old Faithful was just one mile ahead. After a mile I turned off the road to Old Faithful, which I missed erupting by a few minutes when I stopped to use the bathroom. I wondered if I should wait for the next eruption, but instead I returned to the main road and headed southeast to West Thumb Junction.

I had walked about four hours when I reached the Continental Divide, elevation 8,262. What I knew of the Continental Divide was this —water that falls on the west side of the divide drains to the Pacific Ocean. Water that falls on the east side drains to the Atlantic Ocean.

What I didn't realize was that the divide wasn't some large, straight rift, rather that it moved all over the place, and I ran into two more Continental Divide signs as I walked. That night I camped illegally, hidden in the dense forest just 50 yards from the road.

My third day in Yellowstone, I reached West Thumb—which received its name from its thumblike projection of Yellowstone Lake—and began my trek around the lake's western perimeter. The scenery was beautiful and the air was crisp and sweet, similar to my walk through Washington over Highway 2.

The day proceeded without incident until I had an experience that every car-driving tourist in Yellowstone hopes for and anyone in the wild prays not to have; I encountered a grizzly. I had stopped to eat my lunch when the bear walked into a clearing about thirty yards in front of me.

I slowly reached into my pack for my gun, praying that I wouldn't have to use it, as the advantage definitely belonged to the bear.

I had once seen a PBS documentary on a bear-mauling incident, and I came away with information that, at that moment, was rather unsettling: the bear's metabolism is so slow that it can still run two- to three-hundred yards after a direct shot through the heart. With a small-caliber handgun the chances of a direct hit on a moving bear's vital organs—especially with my untrained hand—was infinitesimally small, and with a round as small as a 9-mm bullet, it might only serve to make the animal angrier.

I'm not certain whether or not the bear saw me, though I assumed it had at least smelled my presence. It lingered in my area for a tense few minutes, clawed at a tree, and then lumbered off. I don't think I breathed until then. I waited ten minutes to make sure it was gone, then I walked back out to the road and continued my trek.

That afternoon I walked past acres of forest that had been burned, leaving black, ashen remains on trees and the heavy scent of sulfur in the air. It wasn't until after dark that I reached greenery again. I knew from road signs that I was finally near the park's east entrance, but I was exhausted, so I hiked into the forest and made camp. The bear was still on my mind, and I spent an uneasy night, waking at every snap of twig or coyote howl.

As it turned out, I had camped less than a mile from the East Entrance gate. I crossed the Yellowstone River on Fishing Bridge, which, appropriately, was lined with fishermen, then stopped at the Yellowstone General Store.

Even though I had officially left the park, I wouldn't have known it if it weren't for the signage, as the road led into Shoshone National Park. At lunchtime I sat down with a sandwich and looked over my map. By adding a couple extra miles to my daily routine I could reach my next destination in three days: Cody, Wyoming.

CHAPTER
Forty-nine

If a man cries in the wilderness and
no one hears him,
does he make a sound?

Alan Christoffersen's diary

Cody, Wyoming, was named after the famous (or infamous, depending on what biography you read) William "Buffalo Bill" Cody. Cody was a frontiersman and showman who brought the romance of a dying Wild West to wild easterners and beyond, including the crowned heads of Europe. His Wild West show was so popular that it was even said to have improved relations between the United States and Britain.

Cody, who was a frontier scout and a natural self-promoter, began as a fictional character in the day's dime novels after the publisher Prentiss Ingraham discovered the public's voracious appetite for all things Western—a role the real William Cody stepped into like comfortable cowboy boots.

I arrived in Cody around 9 P.M., walking in darkness for the last two and a half hours—something I usually avoid since snakes sometimes like to stretch out on the warm asphalt at night. I had covered more than 30 miles that day—driven on by the lights of the city. I wanted a warm room, a soft bed, a long, hot shower, and a meal I didn't have to unwrap.

The freeway turned into Sheridan, the main street through town. Cody is a real cowboy town. We sometimes think of cowboys as remnants of our nation's past, forgetting that they're alive and well—or at least alive. Cowboys are a race as distinct as any I've encountered in my travels, with their own language, culture, history, literature, and costumes—a hat, Wrangler jeans, boots, and big belt buckles, the larger the better. They have their own walk as well, a little bowlegged and stooped, as if their backs hurt.

About a mile and a half into town I stopped to eat at the Rib & Chop House. My meal was large and heavenly. My server's name was Kari, a pert, fresh-faced nursing student who looked as out of place in the Cody population as I did. She was also the first person I'd talked to in days.

I took my time eating and when I finally stood, my thighs cramped up. I walked (limped) a few blocks down to the Marriott and booked a room. There was a quilters' convention in town, and the hotel was crowded with quilters and cowboys, which seemed culturally congruent.

That night I spent a long time soaking in the hotel's hot tub. When I first arrived, there was another man in the tub, not surprisingly a cowboy, and he wore his hat. He tipped it at me as I stepped into the water. I pulled off my T-shirt and threw it onto a nearby vinyl chair then settled into the bubbling water.

"Howdy," the cowboy said.

"Howdy," I said back, not knowing why I was speaking "cowboy."

He pointed to the scars on my abdomen. "Look like yer dun yerself a li'l fight'n."

"Wasn't much of a fight," I said, sinking down into the water.

"Me too," he said. He rose up a little from the water, revealing the scar from a knife wound, a slash, across his sternum. "Yer should'a seen the other feller," he laughed.

I closed my eyes, hoping he might just let me relax.

"Where yer frum?"

"Seattle."

"Fishin' or passin' threw?"

I looked at him for a moment, then replied, "I'm here for the quilting convention."

"Oh," he said. He pulled the brim of his hat down and sunk to his chin in the water. A minute later he got out of the tub and left the spa.

I slept well that night, though I had an unsettling dream. I was walking down a long stretch of highway, as forlorn as any as I'd passed through, when I saw a woman walking alone ahead of me. It was McKale. I shouted to her, and she turned back briefly but said nothing and kept walking. I kept walking faster until I was running, but she just increased her speed to match mine. She was always just within sight and just out of reach. I woke, the sheets wet with perspiration.

CHAPTER
Fifty

The Wild West has never been so dull.

Alan Christoffersen's diary

I spent the next day resting. I had a big breakfast in the hotel's restaurant, then watched a movie on the pay-per-view—one of the *Bourne* movies. You really can't go wrong with Matt Damon.

I took everything out of my pack, releasing a stale, moldy smell into the room. I discovered a completely withered and black banana, a moldy deli roll, and a couple of half-eaten energy bars.

I washed my pack in the shower-bath, then left it open to breathe next to the window. I laid out my map, then, based on my route, compiled a shopping list on a hotel notepad. I was still several weeks out from Rapid City. Miles to go.

I traced my route with the plastic cap of a hotel pen. I would stay on I-90 until I reached a fork in the road about 280 miles east of Cody. I could travel north on Interstate 90 up through Spearfish and Sturgis, South Dakota, or take the smaller road south to Custer, South Dakota. It was about the same distance either way. The upside of heading south was that the roads were smaller and less busy. The downside was fewer amenities. I elected to go south. I put away my map and went grocery shopping.

As I left Cody the next morning, I felt weighed down, not just because I had stocked up on so many supplies, but because my soul felt heavier. The two-lane highway, like my life, seemed to stretch out to nothing. The land was agricultural, with large, fallow fields for planting or grazing —the patchwork I had looked down on from plane rides in my previous life.

The next two weeks through southeast Wyoming I felt as if emotionally I had taken a giant step backward. I would detail my various stops, but it would only bore you—I know because it bored me. I stopped writing in my journal. I stopped shaving. I stopped caring.

There were few towns on my walk, the largest being Gillette, Wyoming, with a population of about 20,000. The city calls itself the "Energy Capital of the Nation" and is abundant with natural resources: coal, oil, and methane gas. The town was dirty and gray, and I was more eager to leave it than I was to arrive there. There was a desolation of spirit that was as palpable as the cigarette stench of every restaurant I entered. Wyoming is one of the last holdouts on public antismoking laws, and smoking is as much a part of the culture as license-plate-sized belt buckles. Simply put, every public place in the city stinks of ten thousand cigarettes.

I've known people from Wyoming (one of my agency's media reps comes to mind), and I've heard tale of its rugged beauty and friendly, folksy inhabitants, but honestly, in this part of the state I didn't feel it. Wyoming depressed me to the core, though I'm certain that it's likely that my feelings were less a result of the actual state than my state-of-mind—my pain stemming from a combination of loneliness, physical discomfort, and the unchanging landscape.

Each day the postwinter, gray-yellow terrain that surrounded the highway appeared pretty much the same as it had the day before, and my toil felt like that of the Greek Sisyphus, each day pushing a stone to the top of the hill only to have it roll down again.

Nicole's former landlord, Bill, had said something to me a few days before his death that I now had reason to recollect. Without his wife, he said, his life felt like a walk through a desolate and forlorn wilderness. Each day was a pointless trek with no one who cared, no one to ask him about his day, his thoughts, his colitis.

That's exactly how I felt. Perhaps this walk through Wyoming was the perfect metaphor for my life without McKale. As I wrote once before, I was lonely but not alone—my companions were despair, loneliness, and fear. And they were a talkative bunch.

During these difficult days I called my father once and Falene twice. My father spent a half hour telling me about his last golf game and, for the first time in my life, I relished each word. Falene could sense my discouragement and she lifted my spirits greatly. She even offered to drive out, an invitation I came seriously close to accepting. But an internal voice told me to push on through the shadow lands alone, that I would have to walk them sometime—if not now, then later.

So I trudged on, and the more I walked, the more difficult it became. My mind began to work against me, to focus on the hard and the despairing, to see only the shadows and not the sun. A thousand times I relived the final days and minutes of McKale's life. Worst of all, I began to doubt.

What was I doing out here? This was an insane idea to walk across the country—there was nothing here, and nothing at my destination was waiting for me. My body ached as much from depression as from the elements, but not nearly as much as my heart. I knew that I was in a bad way, but in dark moments like these, it's not what you know, it's what you feel. And I felt hopeless. I doubted my motives. I doubted that I would ever finish my walk. Then, in one especially dark moment, I doubted my wisdom in not swallowing the bottle of pills. If it hadn't been for what I'd soon find in South Dakota, I don't know how much longer I could have held on.

CHAPTER
Fifty-one

I spent the night in Custer, South Dakota.
I hope I have better luck here than he did.

Alan Christoffersen's diary

On my thirteenth day from Cody I reached
Wyoming's eastern border. Crossing from
Wyoming into South Dakota was like the
moment Dorothy emerged from her relocated
Kansas home into the magical, Technicolor
world of Oz.

The roads I walked were no longer rough, pot-
holed asphalt, but smooth, paved concrete of a
pinkish hue. In eastern Wyoming the dingy,
prefab homes I passed were surrounded by
their own weedy landfills of rusted cars and
abandoned household appliances, while just over
the border the land was green and lush, with
well-kept farms and beautiful red barns.

By evening I entered the town of Custer and
my spirits lifted some. I ate dinner at a pizzeria
(I downed an entire medium-sized pizza myself)
and found a warm, bright hotel crowded with
tourists excited to see Mount Rushmore and the
myriad sites the area offered.

A long row of Harley-Davidson motorcycles

were parked in front of the hotel, presumably on their way to Sturgis, even though the Harley gathering wouldn't officially begin for another hundred days.

I lay in bed the entire next day, melancholy and defeated. I had walked more than a thousand miles and for what? What good had it done? McKale was still gone—and my heart was still broken.

I didn't eat that day. I never left my room, acting the hermit I was looking like. My beard was several inches long, and scraggly.

The second day I was hungry and bored so I forced myself out of bed around noon, I ate lunch at a Subway sandwich shop, then took a shuttle to see the nearby Mount Rushmore and Crazy Horse monuments.

When I first arrived at Mount Rushmore, the monument was concealed by clouds, which seemed appropriate for my life, and since the shuttle didn't return for an hour I waited at the visitors' center and gift shop, where they had plastered the four presidents' faces to everything conceivable, from playing cards to chopsticks.

Then I heard someone shout, "Look, you can see them!" and I walked outside as the clouds dissipated and the faces were revealed: Washington first, then Jefferson, Roosevelt, and Lincoln.

You hear it all the time: Mount Rushmore isn't

as big as you think it's going to be, but even in my state of mind the memorial was phenomenal.

All art intrigues me, and something on this scale had an especially powerful effect, so I hiked the trails beneath the mountain and lingered around the visitors' center and museum until it was beginning to get dark. At that late hour I found myself debating whether to just head on back to my hotel or over to the Crazy Horse Memorial.

Frankly, Crazy Horse was an aside for me. I knew little about the monument, except that it was an incomplete statue of Chief Crazy Horse, someone I didn't know or care anything about. It certainly couldn't compare with the majesty of Mount Rushmore. But in the end, curiosity won out and I took the shuttle over to the memorial. I didn't anticipate the profound effect it would have on me, my life, and my walk.

CHAPTER
Fifty-two

Some men see mountains as obstacles.
Others as a canvas.

Alan Christoffersen's diary

The Crazy Horse monument was started in 1948 by a Polish-American sculptor named Korczak Ziolkowski. Korczak was born in Boston in 1908 to Polish parents and orphaned at the age of one. He spent his life being shuffled through a series of foster homes in poor neighborhoods. Though he never received formal art training, in his teens he worked as an apprentice to a shipmaker and began to demonstrate his skill in carving wood.

He created his first marble sculpture at the age of twenty-four, a bust of judge Frederick Pickering Cabot, a hero to foster children in the Boston area and the man who encouraged Korczak's interest in art. In 1939, Korczak moved to the Black Hills of South Dakota to assist in the creation of the Mount Rushmore Memorial.

Less than a year later, Korczak's marble sculpture of Ignacy Jan Paderewski, pianist, composer, and prime minister of Poland, won first prize at the New York World's Fair. Shortly afterward he was approached by several Lakota

Indian chiefs who asked him to build a monument honoring Native Americans. Chief Henry Standing Bear wrote Korczak, "My fellow chiefs and I would like the white man to know the red man has great heroes, too."

Korczak accepted the project and began research and planning for the sculpture. Three years later the project was put on hold while Korczak enlisted in the United States Army. He was wounded on Omaha Beach during the invasion of Normandy.

After the war Korczak moved back to the Black Hills and began his search for a suitable mountain. He thought the Wyoming Tetons would be a better choice than the Black Hills, with better rock for carving, but the Lakota considered the Black Hills a sacred place and wanted the memorial built there.

"The Lakota had no money and no mountain," Korczak said. "But I always thought [the Indians] had gotten a raw deal, so I agreed to do it."

When completed, the monument, a three-dimensional sculpture of the Indian Chief Crazy Horse sitting on a charging steed, will be the largest sculpture in the world, standing 563 feet high—taller than the Washington Monument—and 641 feet long. To put the size of the memorial in perspective, just Crazy Horse's war bonnet would be large enough to contain all the presidents' heads on Mount Rushmore.

Korczak died thirty-four years after starting work on the mountain, the statue far from being completed. His final words to his wife were, "You must finish the mountain. But go slowly so it is done right."

I stared at the mountain for nearly twenty minutes. It started to rain on me and I hardly even noticed. The whole thing was absurd. Colossally absurd. A man with no money, no training, and no heavy equipment, decides to carve a mountain. It was gloriously absurd. In Korczak's impossible quest I found what I was looking for.

CHAPTER
Fifty-three

I asked myself what McKale would
tell me to do and I knew exactly
what she'd say, "Get off your butt,
pick up your pack, and get walking."

Alan Christoffersen's diary

The next morning I lay in my hotel bed looking
at the ceiling. For the first time since I set foot
on my journey, I knew exactly why I was walking. My journey wasn't an escape from my past;
it was a bridge to my future, and each small step
was an act of faith and hope, affirming to myself
that life was worth living.

And with that simple revelation the weight
was gone—the heaviness of my despair and self-
pity. It was time to get on with what I'd committed to do and stop feeling sorry for myself. It
was time to stop asking what I could take from
life and learn what life was asking of me.

I opened my map out on the bed and drew a
path with my finger. It was time to head somewhere warm. Time to move south. My next target
was Memphis, Tennessee.

I shaved, grabbed my backpack, and headed

out of the hotel. I was committed again to my next destination.

As I walked through the hotel's lobby, I noticed an older woman sitting in one of the chairs near the reception desk. She had gray hair, a long woolen coat, and a burgundy silk scarf tied around her neck. She was beautiful, or had been once, and something about her was hard to look away from. She was likewise watching me and we made eye contact. When I was near to her she said, "Alan."

I stopped. "Excuse me?"

"You are Alan Christoffersen?"

I looked at her in surprise. "Yes."

"Do you know who I am?"

Something about her looked familiar. After a moment I said, "No."

"Are you sure?"

Then, as I stared into her eyes, I realized who she was. Before I could speak, she said, "I've been looking for you for weeks."

EPILOGUE

We are all in motion. Always.
Those who are not climbing
toward something are descending
toward nothing.

Alan Christoffersen's diary

What my father said about mountains is true. We climb mountains because the valleys are full of cemeteries. The secret of survival is to climb, even in the dark, even when the climb seems pointless. The climb, not the summit, is the thing. And the great don't just climb mountains, they carve them as they go.

Korczak's dream was an impossible one—that one man could sculpt a mountain. I can only imagine the barbs and insults of Korczak's critics, and he had galleries of them. "You're crazy, a fool, you'll never do it," they sang from their low places and half-dug graves. "The statue will never be complete."

But Korczak knew better than to listen to the ghosts in the cemeteries. Every day he climbed his mountain, and with a chisel here, a blast there, he moved tons of stone as his dream emerged from the mountain.

Korczak knew he'd never live to see his work

finished, but this was no reason to stop. As he lay dying, he was asked if he was disappointed to not see the monument completed. "No," he said, "you only have to live long enough to inspire others to do great things."

And this he did. As the mountain took form, the masses began to dream too. And they began to move. Today millions come from around the world to see Korczak's mountain, and a professional crew works year-round to move the dream forward. It is no longer a question of *if* the statue will be completed, only when.

But Korczak's greatest legacy is not a public one, the massive stone mountain that he conquered, but the mountain he first conquered in himself—a mountain that he climbed alone—and in this we can all empathize. For there are moments in all lives, great and small, that we must trudge alone our forlorn roads into infinite wilderness, to endure our midnight hours of pain and sorrow—the Gethsemane moments, when we are on our knees or backs, crying out to a universe that seems to have abandoned us.

These are the greatest of moments, where we show our souls. These are our "finest hours." That these moments are given to us is neither accidental nor cruel. Without great mountains we cannot reach great heights. And we were born to reach great heights.

Every one of us is faced with a task equal to

Korczak's, one as gorgeously absurd—to chip away at the stone of our own spirits, creating a monument to light the universe. And, like Korczak's monument, our task will not be completed in our lifetime. And in the end we will find that we were never sculpting alone.

Korczak said, "I tell my children never forget that man is not a complete being in himself. There's something greater than he that moves him."

I don't honestly know if I'll ever reach Key West, but I do know that I will never give up. And, when I take my final step, whether or not I made my destination doesn't really matter, because in the end I will be a different man than the one who left Seattle. I was never carving a mountain. I was carving myself.

Dear Reader,

As you likely know by now, I write with the hope of improving the world. In *Miles to Go*, I included the character of Kailamai to highlight the important issue of foster youth aging out of care. The Kailamai in my story is partially based on a real young woman. And, like the Kailamai in my story, she's full of hope and gratitude. My daughter Jenna has helped Kailamai write her incredible story. To download her true story go to www.richardpaulevans.com and click the Kailamai link. All of the donations for this story will go to help this young woman reach her dreams.

I want my readers to know that the challenges of youth aging out of foster care are very real: Research from the Pew Charitable Trusts shows that 6 out of 10 youth aging out of the foster care system will be homeless, incarcerated, or dead within the first two years. Most youth aging out of the foster care system lack the essential skills, resources, and support to live a safe and independent life.

GO-Mentor is a collaboration committed to creating programs and offering services that effectively improve such outcomes. GO-Mentor includes the Youth Mentor Project, the School of

Life Foundation, and the National Crime Prevention Council, home of McGruff the Crime Dog®.

To contribute financially to the exciting GO-Mentor initiative, please visit www.ncpc.org or write the National Crime Prevention Council, 2001 Jefferson Davis Highway, Suite 901, Arlington, VA 22202. To learn more about GO-Mentor or to volunteer, please visit www. go-mentor.org. Thank you for your help in building brighter futures for youth aging out of foster care.

Richard Paul Evans is the author of the number-one bestselling novel *The Christmas Box*. Each of his novels has appeared on the *New York Times* bestseller list; there are more than 14 million copies of his books in print. His books have been translated into more than twenty-five languages, and several have been international bestsellers. He has won two first-place *Storytelling World* awards for his children's books and the *Romantic Times* Best Women's Novel Award. Evans received the *Washington Times* Humanitarian of the Century Award and the Volunteers of America National Empathy Award for his work helping abused children. Evans lives in Salt Lake City with his wife, Keri, and their five children.

To learn more about The Walk series or to join Richard's mailing list and receive special offers and information please visit:

www.richardpaulevans.com

Join Richard on Facebook at the Richard Paul Evans fan page www.facebook.com/RPEfans

Or write to him at: P.O. Box 712137 • Salt Lake City, Utah • 84171

Center Point Publishing
600 Brooks Road ● PO Box 1
Thorndike ME 04986-0001 USA

(207) 568-3717

US & Canada:
1 800 929-9108
www.centerpointlargeprint.com